Title Page

Copyright

Dedication

Synopsis

Prologue

MW01656825

TWICE THE DEMISE

By Maureen Joseph

Twice The Demise

Copyright © 2019 Maureen Joseph

Ebook and paperback book cover painting and design by abstract artist: Chucrallah Fattouh

https://instagram.com/chucrallahfattouhofficial?utm_source=ig_profile_share&igshid=2aeiairveoo8

All rights reserved.

This book is a work of fiction. Names, characters, and incidents are either products of the author's imagination or are used fictitiously. Any resemblance to actual events or persons, living or dead, is entirely coincidental.

This ebook is licensed for your personal enjoyment only. This ebook may not be re-sold or given away to other people. If you would like to share this book with another person, please purchase an additional copy for each recipient. Thank you for respecting the hard work of this author.

Dedication to

Mom, I hope I did you proud- I miss you terribly

Dad, Master of Our Universe, Artist and My Inspiration, I Love You

Huda Jreidini, Teacher, Friend, Mentor, Muse

SYNOPSIS

Polly Deuce is not your average undertaker. She loves MP3 players and is somewhat a luddite. She's lived a non-eventful life in her little goth bubble till her childhood best friend, Michael Nabakov, turned her world upside down. For many years, he had managed to keep his identity and motives under wraps. Polly is caught between her guilt with the familiarity of Michael's presence and a strange yearning for his dark pursuer.

Prologue

How many times can a person die? Metaphorically? Literally? Dying metaphorically is never-ending hell; dying literally happens only once. Or so I thought. Everything I knew disappeared in an instant. My faith in science and religion was shaken.

A black weight was dragging me down and down, washing over me like a subtle wave. I was expecting to see the cliché 'white light at the end of the tunnel', but then I didn't. Was Nietzsche, right? Was there such a thing as annihilation? If this was it, then boy was it peaceful.

1

The smell of the green grass was so lulling. I loved the smell of petrichor. It was another rainy August day. My mom, sister and I hadn't bothered to move. The only thing I could hear was the sound of the pitter patter of rain on the leaves of the trees and the soft sensual rustle of the bushes. Small puddles started to form over some plots.

My mom sat back and enjoyed the trickling of the rain on her olive skin. Although her eyes were closed, it looked as if she were crying. A bird fluttered over her head and she laughed. "Guess the bird thought my hair was a nest; that is why you need to brush your hair", she tittered, "or they'll think that your head is some kind of refuge from the rain." My mom had rather curly hair, which stood like a semi-afro. My sis had inherited the same type of wacky hair. I had my father's boring straight hair which tangled if some wind blew through it. I opened a pack of Twinkies and gave one to my sister. It always took me 15 minutes to finish it because I was allowed one piece of highly-processed-over-the-top-sugary dessert twice a week. Sugar tends to get me hyper. My mom waited patiently for me so that we could pack up and go home.

We almost missed the bus. I saw a bi-racial couple sitting across from us. They were cute. The old couple next to them didn't think so. The late 80's still had its issues. She looked Asian-Caucasian, dressed in black and hot pink, very punk. I wished I could have had her mohawk, unlike my boring ever so long hair. He was Black. He had the most beautiful brown eyes. He had a boxer nose. Maybe his mother was Irish. He was wearing a crisp blue shirt and boot-cut jeans. I started imagining their life together. What their domestic life would be like. I thought that they would have gorgeous children. I imagined them walking into church on Sunday with two very beautiful children.I snapped out of my daze as we got to our stop.

It was a short walk home. My father greeted us as we came in. I was glad that he had fixed my bike. I had a *boy's bike*, as everyone called it. It was a burgundy Chopper with dark blue stripes on the side. My father never dressed me in pink. Thank God for that. I could never imagine myself riding a pink bike with pink tassels; or, even worse, a white wicker basket with pink flowers attached. That was an eight on my barf-o-meter.

My dad made the best shish kebabs in the oven. He really knew his way around the kitchen. My mom was simple in her way of cooking, but she made the best tacos. You'd think the woman was Mexican if she knew any Spanish. She could've passed off as a Latina. My dad had white skin and reddish stubble on his face. I used to think he was part Leprechaun - well, an abnormally tall Leprechaun.

After dinner, I went back to my bedroom. My sister and I had always shared a bedroom. She was making a papier mache man. I sat on the windowsill and gazed outside. I was waiting for my mom to finish the dishes so we could get out our coloring books. Coloring books were my mom's favorite pastime. I think she enjoyed them more than we did. She used to keep them on the top shelf in our bedroom so we wouldn't wind up ripping them, God forbid. My mom entered the room with our oversized box of Crayola crayons. Dad brought in the magic-markers that smelled like raspberry. We colored for more than one hour. By then, dad had drawn three tattoos on my sister, and I had sniffed too many raspberry markers. Papier mache man had become papier mache woman.

Come nightfall, I sometimes became hyper. My brain went into over-drive. Even thoughI was eight and didn't have sweets after five in the evening, I sometimes still had trouble sleeping.

My mom had finished reading to me. Her plump lips kissed me good-night on my forehead. I dozed off after that. At 1 a.m., I was sitting on my dad's lap. He was talking to me, but I couldn't comprehend what he was saying. I was incoherent. I had been sleepwalking again. I couldn't go back to bed. My mom made me a glass of warm milk. I finally dozed off at 3 a.m.

"Ouch!" Tears streamed down my hot cheeks. I hated when mom brushed my hair in the morning. It was torture. My hair was always two inches longer when she finished. Instant length! That's an infomercial I would've loved to see. Or, I could've joined the circus and my mom would've been the magician. People would've oohed and aahed at how she was able to grow my hair two inches in five minutes! But then again, that would've been one painful show for me.

It was Saturday morning and we usually went to the supermarket to run errands. I loved going to the supermarket. My sis always sat in front of the shopping cart and I practically just followed my mom like her shadow, watching her as she made choices of what to buy and which brands were overrated. There were many things I still couldn't read and it was frustrating. For instance, those big words with two or three consonants one after the other. What was that about? I learned about many countries while shopping with my mom. My sister, who was six and a half, tried to pronounce Columbia as my mom was helping me read the label on a can of ground coffee.

Suddenly, someone grabbed my sister from the cart; she cried at first then giggled. It was Uncle James. He gave my mom a hug while holding my sister to his side, then he picked me up and walked us to the lobster tank. I loved Uncle James. He always appeared as if from nowhere. He offered to drive us home. My sis and I sat in the back seat and my mom was in the seat next to the driver's. Uncle James used to drive extra slow when we were with him in the car. He also used to put my mom's favorite rock band on the stereo as well. They were both metal heads.

My sister tried to sing along but couldn't keep up with the black clad musicians. It was fun seeing her make up her own language during her sing-a-longs.

I fell asleep to the thrumming of the engine. I rarely fell asleep in cars, but I was fatigued. I woke up after a while with motion sickness. When the car came to a halt, I opened the door and threw up. I should never daydream in a moving car. I loved to daydream, except there was no rewind button. There were no capture or snapshot features. I pulled myself together and got out of the car. My dad hugged my sister and me. It started to rain again. We all got wet, except for my mom who was resting peacefully in a hearse - in her casket.

2

The church was full of mourners and fashionistas. If it weren't for the casket, you'd probably think you were at a cross between a burlesque show and Cher's boudoir. Why would someone need so much jewelry for a funeral? My mom had many friends from the LGBTQ community. She was a God-fearing woman who would never judge anyone by their color, creed, religion or sexual orientation. She considered acceptance to be much more difficult than forgiveness. I truly understood what she meant by that. You see, to forgive, you'd have to get hurt by someone, go through this anger phase, forgive them, and then get over it. But accepting someone for who they are is much more difficult because they may practice a lifestyle which goes against all your beliefs. I found it amusing when someone was 'offended' by a transgendered person, for instance. Why would this person be offended? It's that person who's under the pressure of being accepted by society. Like my mother used to say: "It is none of our F-ing business as long as no one gets hurt."

I got a strong whiff of someone's perfume as they passed by. Never knew you could order perfume by the gallon. My mom's four closest friends stood like statues. You couldn't tell if they were grief-stricken or trying to mimic department store dummies. Uncle James was wearing a Gucci suit. Some men bought cars, he bought high-end garb. He was neither gay nor metrosexual. He unapologetically liked expensive suits. No labeling, if you don't mind.

I sat at the first pew on the right side, first row. The casket was on my exact left. I glanced at one of the hand-painted icons of the Virgin Mary. I lifted my left hand involuntarily and touched the cold mahogany casket. It took me a few seconds to give my brain the signal to turn my head to the left as well. I couldn't. One of the few times I asked my brain for something and... nothing. I'm never talking to it again. A warm hand touched my right hand.

"It's exactly what you ordered. It's beautiful. Come on, you can do it. Turn your head." I was glad to hear her voice. It was finally great to have serenity with a capital S. Serenity, my best friend, was one of the wisest people I ever knew. I was her worst half and she was my best half. She didn't have an evil bone in her body, and was very ethical and very moral. She was the big sister and the occasional sanity I never had.

I finally took a look to my left. There it was, an army of angels not even acknowledging my presence. They were staring at each other and having telepathic conversations. They resembled a painting you'd probably see at The MET. Their eyes were facing up and their lips were slightly parted. Some were holding French harps and trumpets; others simply had sashes and wings. Their faces had more of a citrine than bronze color to them - just the way I ordered them. I walked to the other side to face the foot of the casket, and there it was, what I had been dreading: a plaque with her name on it.

I ran my fingers over the engraved letters - Cherie. I was amazed by the calligraphy. My mom had fabulous handwriting and she used to free-lance as a calligraphist. They used her signature C for her name. There was no maiden name or last name on the plaque, precisely the way she would've wanted it. My father never really cared about such formalities. She was like his private singer or artist, just like Cher or Madonna; her first name was her identity. It was funny when she filled out forms and always forgot to put in her last name. She'd tell whoever was responsible for the paperwork: "I don't need a last name! Don't you know who I am? I'm Cherie!" It was funny making people think that they weren't hip enough to know the latest artist. They'd then wing it and say: "Oh, yeah! Didn't you have that song...umm...what's it called?" My mom would make up a name and say: "Bada bing bada boom!" It was funny yet embarrassing when the lady filling out the forms for your mom would be crushing on her.

Serenity got up and came to my side and said: "You did one hell of a job putting this all together, kiddo. You should do this for a living, not to sound morbid or anything." It wasn't a morbid thought at all. I could see all the purple pink lilies and pink and white roses at the altar. There, next to them, was a picture of my mom in a bronze vintage frame. It was my favorite picture. She was wearing a beige top with a hunter green bolero. She had her favorite plum purple lipstick on. My eyes watered a bit. There were votive candles on all the banisters. I made sure that the votive candles were wrapped in green lace and purple ribbons. Julia was sitting at the church organ. Uncle James was tuning his guitar to my father's cello. My sister had her loyal triangle for all intents and purposes - like using it as an occasional boomerang to shut someone up. I could tell she had a few people on her mind now. Our relatives weren't in her cup of instant coffee.

The church was full and our little death quartet played a classical version of *I Still Love You* . I couldn't believe the number of lace-trimmed handkerchiefs moving around. The priest rambled on and on. I started wondering how his burgundy cloak would look with my black dress. I'd have to add some lace onto that stiff collar. I tried to think about anything - anything but the fact that my mother was lying in a box next to me. When the ceremony was over, I tried to pry the plaque off her casket - Serenity stopped me. She didn't want me ruining my nails. The service finished with Metallica's *Nothing Else Matters* .

We didn't have an open casket service. That was my father's only wish. People went to the reception area. My father asked the priest to open the casket. I took my sister and left the church. I wanted the last memory of my mom to be of her with plum lipstick. Her four best friends stayed behind as well. It was time to lay my mother to rest. The family mausoleum was a couple of minutes away from the church. It was on church property. We walked there with the priest chanting. There were four people carrying my mom's casket; Gene Simmons, Terry 'Hulk' Hogan, Tina Turner and Ron Perlman. It was extraordinarily touching that my mom's clients, friends and people from the LGBTQ community, decided to dress up as her favorite idols. A stream of tears washed down my face. Serenity never left my side. My sis and dad were walking hand in hand. Uncle James was leading the crowd.

I didn't want to look at the mausoleum. I couldn't see because my eyes were always misty and my head was pretty much buried in Serenity's chest. I must ask her what perfume she had on that day. My father and sister entered the mausoleum where they said their good-byes to our Cherie. My sister cried hysterically as Gene Simmons tried to comfort her. There was a huge lump in my throat and I couldn't bring myself to verily cry. I thought I was going to stop breathing. It began to drizzle and Tina Turner started belting out *I Can't Stand the Rain* . Everyone sang along. It was a good thing that Ron Perlman didn't leave his day job as a lawyer; he had a crappy voice. Serenity glanced at me in agreement.

We all went back to the reception area. My sister sat down looking glum. People assumed that she was devastated - of course she was. Yet that glum look was the look that she needed her best friend Jack. She went to the bar and poured two glasses; one for her with five ice cubes and a neat one for my dad. Serenity carried my Russian friend in my loyal flask in her bag. She always carried sizable bags and didn't typically like me putting my junk in them as well. I hated carrying big bags. Only she made an exception today for 'our' VIP bar. I had a few sips and then remembered that I should go pay the rest of the money to the caterer. I left the reception area and walked out into the rain. The caterer's van was parked in front of the church's entrance. I saw the back of a tall robust girl, with quite longish red blondish hair, packing up aluminum plates in the back of the van. Her back was still facing me as I walked towards her.

I took the money out of my pocket and tapped her on the shoulder while she was still organizing the raw material on a rack in the van. I cleared my throat. "Excuse me, Miss. I know you're busy, but I wanted to pay you so I could get back inside to my guests." Once the tray of potato salad finally gave in, she turned around. All I could see was her hairy blonde arms and her very flat chest. She reminded me of a girl I once knew in high school. Poor old Natasha, she had tufts of what it seemed like dust bunnies on her skinny arms.

My eyes met her face. It was weird that she was wearing sunglasses while it was raining. What was weirder was not her square jaw, but her Adam's apple.

3

Good God! Was someone posing as a caterer to steal some potato salad? Then it hit me that he was wearing an apron with the caterer's logo on it. "I'm so sorry, but it's raining and I only saw you from behind and ...umm...your hair falls to the small of your back, I mistakenly assumed you were a big girl," I managed to choke out. *And who was stealing food*, I said to myself. He laughed and said: "Since it is raining and I'm a big girl, I'm going to forgive you. I'm wearing knee-length shorts you know. How could you not see my hairy calves?" he grinned. I stood back a bit and saw that he was right. They weren't just hairy, they were muscular. He was wearing steel-toed Doctor Martens similar to mine. He then turned around and rummaged through a loose-leaf notebook. Aha! - Great butt. Note to self: Have mobile camera phone on standby.

He turned back to me and gave me a piece of paper. "This is your balance. I'm not the one who does the accounting. You have to go back inside and hand this to my brother Sandy. He'll sign it after you pay him. This will also serve as your receipt." I took the paper from him and went back into the reception hall. I couldn't help but think *who wears sunglasses in this cloudy weather?* His lips resembled those of a Greek god; they were well-proportioned and plump. If I could just bite his lower lip - Focus! This is the caterer and you're at your mother's funeral. Truth be told, it was rare for me to see someone in the food industry with such long hair as mine. His hair was straight and double-toned, unlike my monotonous brown hair.

I went up to my dad and asked him where Sandy was. For

some reason, he imagined a strawberry-blonde woman with a wrap dress from the seventies. I tried to explain to him that it was a guy. He then scanned the place for a blond dude in heels. My dad was slow today. I took the goblet from his hand and told him that he needed a refill. I gave it to the waiter and tipped him twenty bucks to make sure that my dad wouldn't cheat on goblet number five.

Sandy was talking to Gene Simmons and my sister. Gene Simmons was a famous chef in our city. Gene was giving cooking tips to Sandy. My sister was pulling his pleather tassels so he would zip it. Gene refused to take the hint. I went up to them and excused Sandy from French Cuisine 101. I handed him the paper and the money. He asked: "Who gave you this receipt?" I answered quickly: "Someone wearing sunglasses with long hair next to your van. I think he said that he's your brother."

He grunted, excused himself, and told me that he'd be right back. Sandy had the same hair color as his Ray Ban brother. I hated Ray Bans. Sandy had hazel eyes and dark eyebrows. I assumed that he was the older one since he oversaw the money. Ron Perlman and Uncle James came my way. They were asking me if I wanted all the flowers to be placed at the mausoleum, or if I wanted to donate half of them to the church. I told them whatever my father wanted. My sister wanted all of them at the mausoleum because, in her mind, the church didn't need any more donations. I called out her name and mouthed to her to take care of the flower situation. I still had to deal with the catering. What was taking Sandy so long?

We ran into each other as I was going down the reception hall stairs. "My brother has issues with using his brain sometimes. He gave you the wrong receipt." He chuckled. "Don't be so hard on him. It was raining cats and dogs and he was wearing his sunglasses," I said half-heartedly. He threw a sarcastic glance at me and said: "See what I mean?" After he signed the receipt, the guests were starting to leave. I searched for my dad and sister so that we could go home. It had been a long day and I wasn't able to bear our relatives anymore. The image of the triangle grew more and more vivid as I imagined it ricocheting off each loudmouth's forehead.

My dad was a mess and my sister was too quiet. I loved driving my dad's black Camaro. I popped in a random CD. It was a power metal band. My dad and sis were lightly head banging in slow motion like two newborn zombies. We reached home and the car idled while my sis and dad managed to get out of the car. He had too much to drink and she was dead tired.

Julia and Uncle James had been waiting for us at the house. My father had given him a key ever since he'd offered to help renovate our kitchen. Uncle James worked as a part time interior designer when he was pursuing another passion. It was going to be an anniversary present from him to my parents. The kitchen was white and pristine. Uncle James had installed white marble as countertops and eggshell porcelain tiles. The kitchen appliances were black. I stared at the Samsung fridge my mom had picked out with me one afternoon. The fridge had Swarovski crystals embedded in the handles and it cost an arm and a leg. She saved up to buy it because it was unique - like her. Suddenly, a sunken feeling hit me. My mom never got to see the final result, nor will she ever.

Julia had prepared some coffee for everyone. I was looking through the kitchen window and saw her son, Michael, watering my mom's hydrangeas.

I hadn't seen Michael off-stage in two years. He had been on tour starring as the Nutcracker with a ballet company. He'd studied ballet mostly in Russia. I only got to see him during the summer after high school. We grew up together, and my father was always there when his mother needed help disciplining him. Michael's father died when he was just a toddler. Julia was like an aunt to me, but she didn't like to be called Aunt Julia. She said it made her sound old. My dad poured me a cup of coffee and excused himself to go to his room. It was his non-verbal way of saying thank you to me.

As I was sipping my coffee, I noticed the amount of detail that was put into our cupboard doors. They were made of wood but painted with a white wash matte paint that framed the stained glass. The stained glass was an abstract Victorian calligraphy monogram of my parents' initials. The engraved lilies were wonderful. My chain of thought was cut off by someone pulling my hair. "Rapunzel, want to go to the supermarket? You're out of food."

There was Michael tugging at a lock of my hair. It had been a habit of his ever since we were kids, not to mention the habit of calling me Rapunzel. He used to play the prince who would save me from the high-towered castle. "I'm too tired and it's already 9 p.m. We have cheese, bread, fruit and Greek yogurt for the morning. I don't think my dad and sis are going to wake up anytime soon." He made a mustache over his mouth with my hair and said in a professor-like tone: "How about we go tomorrow morning? I'll bring over some of my mom's muffins and we'll take a stroll on my low rider. I've installed two side compartments which will be enough to carry your groceries. I still have your helmet."

I stared at my cup of coffee and snorted: "I don't mind taking a short stroll to the supermarket on a low rider with a ballerina wearing a pink tutu, but won't that piss off Clarabel?"

He leaned backwards, contemplating a reply to my question. Clarabel was Michael's girlfriend. She didn't like me and I made no effort to like her either. Well, at first, I had no feelings towards her whatsoever, whether negative or positive. I only knew she was Michael's girlfriend and that he had met her during his ballet tour. She was with him in the same company. Her mother raised bees and her father came from a lot of money. I'd always wondered if she ever helped her mom with honeycombs or identifying types of bees. I actually had two B's to identify the prima donna ballerina: Bulimic and Bitchy. She didn't like the fact that Michael was my next-door neighbor, or that we spent summer together when she was back home. Twenty seconds passed before he answered: "We're on a break." I could tell he wasn't too happy about the break. I didn't bother to ask him about the reason. I bet that she busted his chops. He continued to say: "She said that it was either she or Jessy."

I didn't know whether to feel empathy for Clarabel or punch myself. Be as it may, she did give a crap about Michael. But I knew the end to this ordeal: Michael would never give up Jessy. She was his first and only love. It was like no other relationship between a guy and his ride. I could see, like many other girls, Clarabel was going and the low rider was staying. And not like many other girls, Michael knew that I never minded sharing him with Jessy.

I woke up the next morning in the chaise longue in my bedroom. It was very uncomfortable. It was meant to be sat upon and not slept on, as my mother had repeatedly mentioned to me many times. The TV was still on. I must've forgotten to put the sleep timer last night. I removed myself from the chaise and trudged to the bathroom to take a cold shower in an effort to wake up. I then brushed my teeth, combed my hair, and slapped on some moisturizer and a bit of eyeliner and mascara. I regularly washed my hair every three days, but today was an exception. I put it up in a ponytail. I went back to my bedroom and threw on a pair of black low-waist jeans, my AC/DC T-shirt and a black cardigan. As I was deciding on footwear, I heard a light knock on my door.

It was Michael. He smiled and said: "Good morning, Moonlight. Listen, Gene Simmons brought the raw material to make hors d'oeuvres, but he still needs a few ingredients. Your sister and father are going to take care of the drinks and the guests while we grab a quick bite and go to the supermarket." I just stood still and blurted out: "Why the hell are guests coming to our house today? We just buried my mother yesterday. Besides, I can't go barefoot to the supermarket with you." I wholly felt overwhelmed with all the info he tried to shove into my not-so-functional brain. My eyes watered up a bit. Crap! I didn't like looking vulnerable in front of Michael.

"Sshhh...take it easy; you just woke up. Don't be mad, sweetie. It's merely some people coming from out of town to pay their respects. Don't forget, many people couldn't make it yesterday. Gene offered his services to your dad since he was working only the night shift this week at the hotel restaurant. I think we forgot to tell you yesterday at the funeral. And I think you should wear your burgundy Doctor Martens; no steel toe." He winked at me.

"I only saw you during the service and you were sitting way back. I didn't see who you were with, though. Why didn't you come and sit with the family upfront? Or did you need a private invitation?" I opened my shoe closet and got out *his* favorite burgundy Doctor Martens.

"Well, I was with Clarabel and I didn't want to bring her to the front with me." He was staring down at the floor.

I was confused. "I thought you just said that you two were on a break. That it was either she or Jessy."

"That's right, the break started yesterday. I was going by myself, but then she came over and wanted to talk." He gestured two quotation marks with both hands. "She knew that I had a funeral to attend yet decided to become my shadow the whole time. I couldn't even go up to give you a hug. I don't know what's gotten into her. First, it's Jessy, then the following around."

I shrugged. "Well, it's not that I'm not fond of her; we simply don't have anything in common."

He looked insulted, "Nothing in common? What's this ballerina doing here in front of you?" He was grinning now.

"Well, you being the common factor might be the problem. On the other hand, I haven't seen you off-stage in two years. I watch your performance and, you know, catch the next flight back home. Before that, I'd see you in the summer for like six weeks only because she'd be visiting her parents. And don't forget your mom who is usually either traveling with you or vacationing with my parents and their friends in the countryside."

He rolled his eyes and said: "Ok, I got nothing. Clarabel has to learn to cope with things. I mean, she gets to see me more than my mom does. Even when mom is traveling with me, I still spend most of my time with Clarabel. She has to understand that I have a friend with whom I grew up and that I need to see her once in a blue moon." He crossed his arms, proud of his retaliation.

We went downstairs and found a fair-skinned man with a buzz cut making a Spanish omelet. He had set a gorgeous breakfast spread for us. He even placed a few roses in a bud vase.

"Morning, Sleepyhead. What would you like to eat? You guys have an excellent espresso machine. I could make you a cappuccino. Your dad and sis have already had breakfast. So, it's just you, me, Michael and Julia. I don't know if James is coming for breakfast."

It took me a moment to scan my brain. Nope, I didn't know him. Then it hit me: Gene Simmons' daytime look! I told him that Michael and I were going to the supermarket. He handed me a list of French gibberish. Thank God Michael was coming along with me. He learned some French during his many stays for shows in Paris. "Alright then, you have my cell number if you remember anything else." Gene gave me a hug and offered me one of Julia's muffins smeared with herbal cream cheese. I was beginning to like daytime Gene.

There she was, shining too brightly. "Geez Michael, did you dip Jessy in wax over and over? Or does she get varnished every week?" He laughed. "You're just jealous because you can't pull off her look." I nudged him, "Yeah, that's it. I'm jealous of her gloriousness." I sat behind Michael as he pulled the jack stand up. It's a good thing it was cold because that helmet would've shish-kebabed what's left of my brains. He turned around and said: " Open the compartment to your right." I opened it and pulled out a pleather jacket. It had rubber patches on the elbows and torso area. It looked unique. I gave it to him, but he shook his head. "No, that's yours. It's really cold. That's a little something I picked up for you in Paris." I kissed him on the cheek and thanked him.

He took care of the shopping list. I lazily pushed the shopping cart. We looked like a married couple, except that I was the bored-out-of-my-mind husband and he was the know-it-all housewife. When I was out with Michael, everyone stared. You'd probably think from the way he was built that he was into martial arts or something. He was tall and had charcoal hair that fell behind his ears. He had a little mole on the left upper side of his mouth. His nose resembled that of a Phoenician god. He had white skin, though his arms were a bit tanned. He was a handsome guy.

As we walked towards the deli isle, I saw two women staring at us. They were shamelessly snickering, and I could almost hear their exchange of whos and whats. Michael noticed them as well. He wrapped his hand around my waist and put on a show while walking past them with me. He snickered back at them in a melodramatic manner. I laughed my head off. He then kissed my forehead. "Come on, Moonlight. It's not every day you get to see a ballerina and an undertaker go shopping together for stinky French cheese."

4

Guests started arriving in hordes and I was feeling a little better. I actually saw people that I liked. My sister played cocktail waitress and I played silent movie actress. Michael never left my side. Serenity had taken the day off from work just to try out Gene Simmons' cooking. I hope her new employee would be able to cope without her. She owns a vintage bookshop where I used to spend many evenings working when she first started out. Serenity was four years older than I. She had a round face with dark brown eyes, a cherub mouth with three scars on her upper lip, and crimson red hair set in concentric waves. She was one of the rare people I knew with very good posture and over a hundred pairs of shoes, literally. She always thought that I should be an event planner. My father thought that I would make an awesome accountant. Yet, I found my calling with the dead.

I come from a long line of musicians, but I was never able to master an instrument. I didn't have the discipline. Besides, my fingers and brain were never the best of friends. My fingers were always too cocky and my brain was like a college professor from the thirties. I took up a job as the town undertaker after completing a course in Egyptology and getting a degree in Mortuary Science. I gave up my job as an accountant because there had been more talk and less numbers involved for the last couple of years at my job. That's what happens when management wants you to do accounting and take care of happenstances on a weekly basis. I truly loved the idea of being in a tiny cubicle where I didn't have to interact with the undead. Once I was promoted to Cost Accounting, my cubicle felt like the box office.

I was also required to take a few courses before I could get my license.

I love my current job. I am required to transport cadavers to the funeral home where I worked - Roberts' Funeral Home. It was owned by a well-off family who also sold plots from their private cemeteries. One would say they were quite upscale. Uncle James and his brother William were the sole heirs. Uncle James had taken me under his wing and taught me everything he could about the business. I offered to do the accounting in exchange. My mother used to offer second-hand suits and dresses for the deceased. She was a fashion designer and was sometimes stuck with too much apparel. My sister is expected to take over the business now. My dad was not involved in the business but worked as a forensic sketch artist for the police, and occasionally for the F.B.I. I was the only non-artistic person in the family - Thank God for that.

Michael was nice enough to fetch me an espresso. I was sleepy. Some old work buddies tried to strike up a conversation with me. Dalilah got married to an accountant; *great*, two accountants, very interesting children. Tom got my job; now he can finally get laid. Ruth, from HR, was having trouble walking in her stilettos.

Last but not least, I was glad to see Tina. She had OCD but was the coolest accountant ever. She was Senior Accountant and antiseptics were her best friend. She was always good company and had a wicked sense of humor. I really missed her. Then there was Joy; he was the manager. He now runs a high-end restaurant. Tina and I were the only people in the office who got along with him. He wasn't a jerk or anything. He was just misunderstood. He had a good heart once you got to know him. He was married and had a baby boy.

The difficult part was that people, although they knew, wanted to to hear again how my mom died. Were they trying to torture me or something? They also wanted to know why we had another funeral home take care of the arrangements. I mean, how was I supposed to take my own mother's body from the hospital to the funeral home where I worked? What about poor Uncle James? Dead people were his other passion as long as they weren't his best friends. People could be so dense. Gene Simmons came into the living room and handed me another list. He needed more things. Too many people had arrived and he was running low. Serenity had offered to take me to the supermarket. Michael stayed behind to help out my sister.

It was an utterly quiet ride on the way there. It was so unlike us to have two minutes of silence together in the car. Serenity seemed pale. We were in the supermarket's parking lot. I was going to ask Serenity to unlock the doors when she stared at me in shock, opened her door and hurled on the ground while still sitting in the car. My door unlocked because she opened hers. I opened the door and ran to the other side of the car with a bottle of water in hand. I could see that the contents of her vomit had pieces of undigested shrimp, bell peppers, yellow spew and some green-looking chunks of I-don't-know what - must be celery.

"Girl, are you ok? What did you eat? What do you want me to get you?" I asked, still very worried.

"What did I not eat? I'm ok. I got carried away with the gourmet cooking. I think the shrimp was a tad chewy. I don't do well with chewy food, you know. And I smelled too much of the Balsamic vinegar, and you know how nauseous the smell of vinegar makes me. But, other than that, he's an exquisite chef. I think he's not gay, though." She took a deep breath and sipped a bit of water.

"Babe, of course he's not gay. He just impersonates Gene Simmons and likes wearing very tight jeans. I have no idea where you got that from."

I could not see the correlation. "Now, I don't know if he's a cross-dresser, but I'm one hundred percent sure he isn't gay. He used to date this blonde bar maiden at the hotel. She was Nicolette Sheridan hot." It was getting weird having a conversation over a puddle of vomit.

"Let's go in. I'm ok. I just need a bottle of club soda and I'll be fine. By the way, I saw Bulimia at the funeral yesterday. You'd think she'd gain some fashion sense by living on and off in Paris. But no, she has to come to a funeral wearing black flats, black stockings and an Arabian princess skirt. How the hell did she think that a tunic would match that? I hope her dancing is better than her wardrobe."

Serenity hated it when people were poorly dressed at any event; formal or informal. She didn't like Clarabel, not because she was a bitchy bulimic, but because she was unjustifiably always plain mean to me for no reason. Serenity thinks that she is jealous of my relationship with Michael. More or less threatened by me. I don't know how she came to that conclusion. But hey, Serenity was very perceptive, so I usually trusted her observations no matter how ridiculous they sounded to me; if I didn't, I would be screwing myself over. Rule number one: Serenity is always right.

I never understood why the produce section was the coldest part of the supermarket. I'd normally have a fart festival over there. It was so damn cold. The frozen food section wasn't even that way. "So, what's the difference between flat leaf parsley and regular parsley?" I asked Serenity as she was filling a plastic bag with Turkey figs.

"Well, the regular one is me and the other one is flat bulimic bitch." She had a villainous grin smeared across her face. It was funny.

"My God, Serenity. What's up with you and her? Why can't you stop talking about her today? I mean she's so thin that she barely takes up a sentence worth mentioning."

She was picking out a stalk of celery. "That's funny!"

I nudged her. "I'm glad you find me so amusing even though I'm feeling so glum."

"Well, you can never make me feel glum. You're the funniest when you're glum and gloomy." She snorted.

We were down to our last item. I checked off each item on the list as I went over them in the shopping cart. Blue cheese, Turkey figs, walnuts, pears, lox, cream cheese, cling film, colored toothpicks (because the wooden ones would have been offensive), celery, and Serenity parsley. The cashier had to be the dirtiest guy I'd ever seen. I don't know if using the term 'dirty' was the right adjective to describe him, more likely crusty. He had a line of crust from his hairline to his jaw line and it elongated to the back of his earlobe. His lips were brownish. It looked as if someone took a monumental dump on this guy. He shouldn't be wearing brown. I backed away from the queue and went to another cashier. I didn't want Serenity tossing her cookies all over me and the groceries.

On our way back, Serenity asked me if I needed to buy some concealer. I knew it was her very subtle way of telling me that I needed a stronger one due to the crescents I was sporting under my eyes due to lack of sleep. We passed by the drugstore and also bought some antacids. The house was full of people. My sis was sitting down engaging in small talk with our cousins. I headed to the kitchen and Gene Simmons was showing Michael just how long his tongue was. Gene Simmons had an impressive tongue. I interrupted them with the crunching sound of the bags on the counter. Serenity helped. Gene and I went upstairs to put on some concealer. He slathered that stuff on without a mirror in less than a minute.

My eyes did look bad. I hadn't slept well in quite a while. I had managed to get five hours of sleep last night. I applied the ivory goo on my bags. I should buy this brand more often. It worked like magic and the puffiness kind of disappeared. *I love you Serenity*. I lay down a bit on my bed for a couple of minutes before heading downstairs. I was gazing at my chaise longue. It took my mother a long time to order it. Something black interrupted my reminiscing, the black pleather jacket that Michael had given me earlier as a present from Paris. I picked it up for you in Paris. He made it sound like he had picked up a pack of Twinkies for me.

Serenity was at the door. "Are you ok sweetie?" sounding concerned.

"I'm ok, I was lying down a bit. That concealer worked like a charm." I sat up.

Just as we were about to leave the room, "Wow, where did you get that jacket?"

"Something Michael picked up for me when he was in Paris."

"Something he picked up for you when he was in Paris!" She mimicked me. "And what did he get bulimic bitch, might I ask? A high caloric carrot?"

"Come on, Serenity, you read too much into things. I mean, when I'm away I always bring something back for him, and you as well. He doesn't think of me that way. Besides, he knew I needed one because I lost my jacket the last time we went clubbing with you, if you remember. Someone stole my jacket and that one was leather, much more expensive." I pronounced the last sentence with complete articulation.

"Who said it was pleather you dim-wit? It's leather. The only pleather parts are the elbow patches, but the rest is genuine leather. He's buying you expensive things without you knowing. Have you ever bought me an eight-hundred-dollar jacket?" She turned and went downstairs to call my sister. I sat down in utter shock. No one has ever bought me something so expensive. I couldn't accept this from him. Michael was making his own money and helping his mother with the mortgage. I mean, how much money would he have to make to splurge on a ridiculous item such as a jacket, and I wasn't even his bulimic bitch. My enunciation bit obviously backfired.

Serenity had dragged my sister from the guests downstairs in order to prove to me once more that she was right. My sister held up the jacket. She observed it and was quick to identify fabric, cut and designer. She said: "Well, the thermal padding is what makes it a motorcycle jacket. The leather corset sewn onto the torso was special ordered. Only the patches on the elbows are padded pleather. I mean, to customize this in such a manner costs as much as the jacket itself. But check out the handiwork on this! It's amazing! Have you noticed that there's faux crocodile leather on the brim of the collar? My God, how on Earth could you afford this?"

I looked at my little sister sheepishly. "I can't afford this. I'm not the one who bought it. Michael picked it up for me in Paris." I tried to make it sound as casual the way he had done earlier.

My little sister held back a chuckle. "Listen to you. No one just 'picks up' an item like that. First of all, that's a limited-edition jacket you've got there. Second, in order to customize and alter it, there is an eight-week waiting list for your order to get through. Last, it's your exact size. This jacket has been made for you. Can't you see? I wonder what he took in order to perfect such measures. By the way, off-the-rack version is worth more than a thousand bucks."

A thousand bucks? What the heck? Come on! Imbecile! Why didn't he just buy me a pair of Doctor Martens? I was in dire need of hunter green ones. I tried not to hyperventilate.

"He's the one who stole her leather jacket!" Serenity cupped her mouth after she realized what she'd said.

"I don't think so. We've been friends since forever. He keeps some of his stuff by me sometimes, and I keep some stuff by him. Michael is not that type of guy. He's crazy about Clarabel, even though she gets on his nerves sometimes."

Before leaving the room, my sister said: "Stuff, not clothes and well-fitted jackets." Serenity was looking smug. How could I have been so stupid? Serenity excused herself to use the bathroom and I went downstairs looking for my dad. It wasn't the time to think about this.

Two days and two hundred hors d'oeuvres later, the house went back to its normal quiet and serene atmosphere sans mother. I went to the kitchen and my father was reading the paper. My sister was fixing breakfast. I practically missed Gene. He had been like our personal cook. I have to pick up something nice for him.

"Dad, I think I should go pick up something for Gene after work today. He was utterly kind and he even did the dishes." My father peeped at me from his paper.

"Sweetheart, are you sure you can go back to work today? You know, with your line of work and all? I have to go down to the precinct to sketch a suspect for a rape victim and your sister has to finish up orders for clients. Julia is going with her to help with organizing the paperwork. We know how badly your sister can screw up orders." He took a sip from his double espresso.

"Dad, it's a job I've been doing for almost three years. I've learned to deal with it. Besides, I can't stay at home anymore. I'm going crazy. So, can you please be a dear father and drive your adult daughter to work like all daddies do?" I pouted my lips.

"Alright, get your things and start the car. Your sis is carpooling with Julia." He folded the paper and went to the living room to get his art supplies.

I went to the driveway, and there was Michael tuning Jessy onto the sidewalk. He came up to greet me. I tried to act cool, but I couldn't. I impatiently huffed and accused him of splurging on non-bulimic bitches. I lectured him and he listened. When I finished he said: "Do I have to give you every detail of every move I make when I decide to get my friend something?"

"So, let me get this straight, you buy your friends ten hundred plus dollars jackets?" I raised my eyebrows. He puckered his lips. I don't think he could've come up with a fast excuse.

"I'm sorry, but I can't accept that. It's too lavish and inappropriate." I stared at him; still no answer from him. I left him there standing and went back into the house. I ran upstairs and got the jacket. I almost stumbled down the stairs and raced through the living room out to the driveway. I handed him the jacket. He wouldn't take it.

"Why are you doing this to me? Is there an appropriate way to give my friend a present? And, no, I don't give my friends ten hundred dollar jackets because most of them read twenty-five dollar books or play three hundred dollar instruments during their leisure time. And who said that it costs that much?" He was the one who was huffing now.

"My sister, or did you forget that she works with fabric, you moron? Take the jacket back and give it Clarabel. When your break ends, she'll have something to cover that tiny body of hers when she's riding with you." I half smiled; he didn't reciprocate.

"She has never ridden with me. This is just a thing that you and I do. No one has ever ridden this bike with me as much as you. It's our thing." Ok, I could see that I was about to make an adult ballerina cry. I didn't like where this was going. I could see that I'd hurt him, and that's something I would never do intentionally.

"I'm sorry, Michael. If it means that much to you." I was staring at the ground.

My dad honked the horn and I gave Michael a peck on the

cheek. I took my jacket and hopped into the car. As we left the driveway, I looked through the visor mirror as Michael's statuesque figure became smaller and smaller.

5

Uncle James was waiting for me at the reception. It felt like yesterday when he was still an interior designer. I vividly remember that he was a big Andy Warhol fan. He didn't look anything like your typical funeral director. He might have switched careers, but he was still the gothic Andrew Eldritch. To be fair, he wore dressy pants instead of jeans to work.

He handed me a list of pick-ups and plot numbers where the crew should dig. We had three funerals set for this week. I got into the company van with our coroner to pick up our first package of the day. Uncle James decided to hire a part-time coroner ever since there was an incident with one of our friendly competitors where one body was in the morgue for a day. The guy turned out to be alive and had post-mortem characteristics which made him appear dead. I know the physiological aspects, but I wasn't a doctor. At this stage, I just bag them and tag them. I was so glad that our new coroner wasn't a woman of many words, my kind of personnel.

We reached the hospital. Morticians enter hospitals from the back side. You don't want to go carrying people in body bags in front of patients and visitors. There, laid in the morgue, a guy in his twenties. He had three gunshot wounds to the chest and pink nail polish on his toenails. I don't want to even know what happened. They hadn't done an autopsy on him because his family was religious or something. I mean, it was obvious how he died - again I am no CSI. I imagined a cult with pink toenails. I rolled the body on a gurney to the back of the van. The coroner and I slid the body onto the fridge. I shut the doors and sent the gurney back in. Pink toes' burial was scheduled at 5p.m. today.

As a mortician, you are required to learn how to prepare a body for burial and how to embalm it. However, Uncle James' family business was expanding quickly and had to break down job descriptions. I generally had to be everywhere. Our embalmer was waiting for us eagerly back at the parlor. I helped him sometimes when he needed an extra pair of hands. His apprentice had been taking too many sick days off because of her allergies. Poor Sarah.

Marc always waited for his cadavers like a Jewish boy on the first night of Hanukkah. When he opened those body bags, he looked like a little kid on Christmas morning. The first thing he noticed as he unzipped the bag was the waxed arms, then the pink toenails. "It seems like his girlfriend was experimenting on him before her husband came home and whacked him."

"Marc, seriously, how did you come up with that?"

"It was in the newspaper. The husband is in jail and the woman suffered a blow to the head." He showed me the newspaper article and pointed to the pictures of the victim's girlfriend and her husband.

"Wow, I'd better go now and dig up his plot. I'll catch you later."

I was so glad it wasn't sunny today. The soil was a bit too moist due to the rain we had for the past three weeks. The crew had set up a tent in case it rained again. You should give the soil a chance to dry up a bit before you can dig six feet deep. I missed my shovel. The calluses on my hands had softened up in the past week from lack of digging. I put on my hat and gloves and started scooping the dirt with the crew. Some family members of the deceased were starting to arrive to make last-minute arrangements. Two hours later, I had a perfect six-foot deep rectangular plot.

I went back to the embalming room and Marc hadn't finished. He was in deep thought. "What's wrong?" I asked.

"I'm wondering if I should remove the nail polish or keep it. We don't have time and he's going to be wearing shoes anyway so..."

"Man, it's 12 p.m. and I think that they want to start their wake now. We have to move him to the reception hall. They're holding the service at the cemetery. Let me help you."

We both dressed Mr. Pink Toenails. We placed him in his satin padded casket. Marc had done a stellar job with the makeup. I rolled the casket on a refrigerated gurney to the hall. His girlfriend had nothing on his widow. Stupid bastard!

After the service, I lowered the casket with the lever. The handle of the lever made the casket as light as a feather. His widow and son wailed with grief. His son was only six years old. I hoped the casket crashed by accident so that his body touched the soil, thus hastening the deterioration process. I didn't understand men. I didn't understand Michael.

I scooped the dirt over the casket. The dirt had dried up and it sounded like it was raining gravel on the casket. Loved ones threw roses into the plot. The priest was reciting final rites. The widow never stopped crying and I just kept throwing dirt on the casket. It felt like I was literally burying a cheating bastard. Uncle James was calming the widow and comforting her son. He was a natural. It started to drizzle a bit, and I had almost finished filling the plot with Angelo's help. He signaled for me to leave because my work was done and he needed to insert the headstone. Angelo was whistling the theme song of The Godfather; the service was over and I needed to pee.

It was time for me to leave. Uncle James had given me an advance on my weekly paycheck because he sensed that I needed the money. My car had broken down the day of my mom's funeral, and I was too stubborn to ask my dad for money. I gave him a peck on the cheek and told him that my dad would be home tonight. They always went out Wednesday nights. I stood outside waiting for Dad to pick me up, when suddenly, I saw a very glossy low rider parked in front of the entrance. Michael was already next to me.

"Your dad got caught up at work with a case and asked me if I could pick you up. My mom and your sister are meeting with a client. Your sis is horrible with taking notes. I think she's hired my mom full-time now. So, it's just you and me." He made it sound like my father had made him take out the trash.

"Umm, thanks Michael. You didn't have to. I'm waiting for Marc to finish up. I'm carpooling with him and Angelo today." I lied my ass off. There was no way he was going to make me feel like an unwanted chore. This was getting too weird, and I was getting very uncomfortable.

"Alright then, have it your way. It's going to pour in a while and you don't want to get caught in the rain while walking to the bus stop." His face was straight.

"I told you I'm carpooling. You can go before it starts to rain on you and your bike. Bikes are not safe in the rain." I hissed at him.

"Says the girl who mostly rides with me on rainy days. I can take a hint. You don't want me around. I understand. But, know one thing. You mean a lot to me, and I would never do anything to jeopardize our friendship, or hurt you for that matter."

I stiffened. "Look, Michael. Since you can take a hint, why don't you take it with you and just leave? Alright?" He stared at me and turned abruptly. It started to pour and Michael disappeared into the dark rainy street. I didn't have an umbrella. I walked to the bus stop. The bus arrived after two cigarette puffs of the lady standing next to me under the leaking shelter. I got on the bus and was surprised to see it basically empty during rush hour. I sat in the middle row next to the window.

My hair was soaking wet. I tried to wring out the water from it. I was going to need a long hot shower. It was a Wednesday, so my dad would've prepared a blue cheese salad and entrecote. That man loved meat, God bless his heart. My sister loved it well-done. I loved it rare, just like my sanity.

I got out my MP3 player and headphones. I know. Who still uses MP3s? But they are so easy to fit in your pocket, especially in my line of work. Alright! It was a gift from Michael and I have had it ever since. I listened to my favorite doom metal songs. There were two boys who were getting off at a stop. My stop would be the next one. I started thinking about what I should get Gene Simmons as a gesture.

The bus doors opened and four men got on. The two boys never left the bus because the four men were carrying AK47s. The boys ran to the back of the bus. The shortest one hit the driver on the head with the butt of the rifle. The driver was unconscious and shorty took control of the bus. The men didn't point their guns at anybody; they just told us not to move or call the police. They headed and aimed towards me, shooting two passengers who were sitting behind me. I knew I was next. One of them walked towards the dead bodies and removed a duffle bag from under the seat. They shot a female passenger in the shoulder for trying to call the police. I just sat still, never removing the headphones from my ears.

The same guy who removed the duffle bag turned towards my seat. He removed my headphones and snatched my MP3 player. I didn't care. I was going to lose it in a month like the other twelve I previously owned. Yes, the other twelve Michael had bought for me every time I lost one. I could see that one of the boys was trying to text someone. I had to think fast and distract the MP3 snatcher.

"Sir, please take whatever you want but leave us alone. You don't want to shoot any more people. Please do what you have to do, but there are children on this bus who just want to get home to their parents."

"Listen, Love, I will shoot anyone who will sidetrack us. So, shut your pie hole and stay put. This way no one gets hurt. We don't want a bullet in that pretty little head of yours, now, do we?" He glared at me.

I wanted to know what was in that duffle bag. I closed my eyes and wished my mother would haunt them and scare them away. But that didn't happen. I could hear the sirens and I saw armed police cars through the window. The boys must've sent a duress message to someone. I was surprised to see the SWAT team afar.

As the hostiles realized what was happening, they turned to shoot around -facing the end of the bus. The MP3 snatcher was still standing next to my seat. He motioned to the other two hostiles to attend to the side windows in case the police started shooting first.

The MP3 snatcher appeared to be aiming at the boys. Only, he wasn't going to use his AK; I heard him cock what appeared to me to be a pistol, maybe a Glock. Without thinking, I got up and smacked him on the head with my messenger bag. He didn't budge. He stood still with the gun in his right hand and shoved me hard to the side window above my seat. I hit my head and felt kind of queasy. I got up again and leaped in front him before he could pull the trigger.

He fell on his back and I fell on him. We were facing each other. I gazed into his eyes; they were immense and radiant green. I put my hand on his ski mask. It was wet and covered in blood. Only it wasn't his, it was mine - gurgling from my mouth. My head dropped to his shoulder as if I were his lover trying to get into his nook. His neck smelled like musky white roses. The metallic redolence of my blood was interfering with my sense of smell. He wrapped his arms around me. I drifted away into the realm of nothing.

6

I was drifting in and out of consciousness. I heard an exchange of gunfire. After what it seemed like twenty seconds, it was all too quiet. I could see shards of glass on the floor. I was still lying on the MP3 snatcher. Why hadn't he moved? An army of boots were in my view. I couldn't breathe anymore. The floor was getting colder. I heard loud voices and commands flying all over the place. I could hear the MP3 snatcher yelling unintelligible words. The pain was excruciating. Tears were flowing down my cheeks.

"The medics are on their way. I'm not supposed to move you. You're not dying on me." He caressed my hair in a way that reminded me of my mother. I tried to keep my eyes open, but the pain overpowered me, hence the blackout.

This was a new kind of headache. Maybe that's how migraines felt like. I wondered about people who suffered from very strong ones. I remembered a professor at school who had to quit mid-semester because of chronic migraines. He was admitted to the hospital a couple of times where they administered morphine drips to keep him from fainting from the pain. I felt bad for Professor Dudy. My mouth was ultradry and I couldn't move my tongue. My nose itched. My eyelids felt like they'd gained a few pounds. They were surprisingly heavy. I wondered if there were any Hollywood diet fads for obese eyelids.

I opened my eyes with great difficulty. I saw red and purple roses. Was I on Marc's slab in the embalming room? My ass was freezing. I tried moving my right hand to no avail. It felt rather heavy. I managed to move my fingers on my left hand and noticed my new jewelry. I had a clamp on my index finger and some wiring wrapped around my wrist like a bracelet. I managed to turn my head a bit to the right and saw a bigger accessory on my other wrist. No wonder I couldn't move it - It was big, shaggy, black, not to mention- heavy. I tried to move my hand again and succeeded. I noticed that the big shaggy thingy was also drooling on my hand. Since when did they let small pooches into the hospital? I couldn't see what breed it was because I was still very groggy. The lump of fur finally moved. No IV needle. Maybe I was on a slab.

The lump of fur moved again. There was an extension, a back of a neck, shoulders and a whole human body sitting on a chair. Mmmm, someone's head had fallen asleep on me. My vision was clearing up a bit. There was a tattoo on the back of the neck but I couldn't tell what it was. I looked up and here was some guy wearing white. Please don't be The Angel of Death or any archetype being! It dawned upon me that I was in a hospital and doctors wore white coats. He approached me and pressed a buzzard next to my bedside. He was looking at a screen and taking notes. The celestial being woke up my visitor who'd used my hand as a pillow. My sleepy visitor was Michael. He stared at me and froze. What was wrong with him? Michael ran out of the room. The guy checking my vitals said: "Hello, Miss Deuce. I'm Nurse Paul. You've been in an induced coma for the past few days.You were badly shot in the abdomen, at very close range. It was a through and through. You underwent two surgeries to repair severed arteries and tissue. If you can understand me, please nod your head."

I nodded my head and something was stinging my neck. I tried to look down to my side but saw nothing.

He tapped my hand and said: "There's an IV drip running from your external jugular which is an EJ PIV. You have small veins."

Another nurse appeared at the door.

"Go fetch Doctor York right now, please." Nurse Paul demanded turning his head back toward me, "We are going to remove your feeding tube. The doctor is on his way." He removed the IV from my neck and started a new one. I honestly couldn't feel the needle puncturing the back of my right hand. Doctor York entered the room with a female nurse.

"Miss Deuce, I want you to take a real deep breath so that we can pull out your feeding tube. Blink once if you understand." I blinked once. I took a deep breath and Nurse Paul and Dr. York managed to pull a long tube out of my mouth. I felt a bit squeamish. The female nurse gave me a sip of water. Michael came back into the room half an hour later, all flustered. He turned to the doctor and told him: "I called her father. He's on his way with her sister."

"Make sure to not overwhelm her, she's in dire need of rest. I must go and phone Mr. Roberts. He wants me to personally deliver the news." The doctor then turned away from Michael and addressed me: "Miss Deuce, if you need anything, Nurse Paul will help you. Just use the buzzard on your left side."

Nurse Paul, Doctor York and the female nurse left the room. Michael went back to the chair next to my bed and held my hand. He just stared at me. Complete silence, not a peep. I managed to utter: "Hi." My voice was hoarse; too bad I couldn't try growling to a doom metal song. "Babe, you had me worried sick. We thought you weren't going to make it. You were in bad shape but you're going to be as good as new. Don't worry; I'm never leaving you again." He looked so serious; someone was ordering a side of Crow's Feet at an early age.

"My head...hurts and...my body feels numb." I was falling back asleep.

"I'm going to call the nurse." He got up from his chair and left the room. My father had arrived with a bouquet of flowers. My sister was right behind him with a big teddy bear dressed in leather and holding a shovel. *Aw, how cute.* Michael had re-entered the room with Nurse Paul. He injected something into my IV drip. My father just kept staring at the wires and at my face. The great thing about Dad; he wasn't melodramatic nor the crying type.

"We've missed you at home kid. Everyone thought that you weren't going to make it, but I never believed for a second that you wouldn't pull through. Baby, you were at the wrong place, at the wrong time. You were very brave trying to save those boys. By the way, they've been visiting you every day. Uncle James offered to pay extra for a private room in the ICU wing; this way he'd make sure you got the best care."

"Tell him 'thank you' for me please."

"I think he's on his way so you'll get to thank him yourself."

"What time is it?"

"It's ten to six." My sister said informatively. "It's night time now. I messaged Serenity and she'll be here at eight. I'm going to leave now and let you rest. I'll be back in the morning with breakfast."

"Okay kid, since Uncle James and Serenity are coming, I'm going to leave you so that you can rest a bit. I'll be back first thing tomorrow at ten with some guys from the precinct." He got up and gave me a peck on my forehead. My sister put the teddy bear next to me. I felt so groggy.

As I was drifting off to sleep, I saw Julia rub my cold feet. I didn't hear her come into the room. "Michael went home to shower and he's coming back. I'm coming with your sister tomorrow morning. Take care, Sweetie." She waved goodbye and turned off the lights.

I finally dozed off. My headache was bearable. The beeping monitor was my night light. I woke up after what felt like an hour feeling pain in my back and stomach. I felt dizzy. I think the painkillers were wearing off. Uncle James was asleep on the sofa and Serenity was, what felt to me, tweezing my eyebrows. She immediately pressed on the morphine pump.

"Remember that pact we once made that we were going to pluck each other's eyebrows and upper lip fluff if we were ever in a coma?" She smiled at me.

I smiled back with a weak "Yeah."

"It's a good thing we made that pact. You've had people in here every day around the clock. I took the liberty of putting some concealer and mascara. I also used a nude lipstick on you. Everyone's been here to see you, even Bulimic Bitch. I think she was pissed because you looked better than her in a coma. Girl, Michael was sitting next to you and you looked like Sleeping Beauty. Prince Charming, Sleeping Beauty and The Wicked Witch." Proud of her unrelated fairy tale analysis, she started filing my nails.

Uncle James woke up and went to the bathroom. He didn't close the door. He just washed his face. He came out yawning; poor Uncle James. He sat next to me on my bed and gave me a big hug. Serenity handed him the eyeliner. He started lining the rims of his eyes.

"There you are. I made Serenity buy this brand. It's the best. Waterproof." he gloated.

"No one could be more masculine with eyeliner than you are." I coughed.

"I offered to get a beautician, but Serenity wouldn't let me. Sorry though, we couldn't paint your nails black or purple - against the rules." He chortled.

"Now, why would you get her a beautician when she has her

best friend to do the job? Besides, I know what she likes. Don't you have to be somewhere? You look awfully tired." She smiled at Uncle James a little too firm.

"Umm...I'm going to call the nurse. Sweetie, I should go now. I may come by tomorrow night. It's been hectic at the parlor. Our temp is just awful." He kissed my forehead and left.

"I may be groggy but I'm not stupid. What's going on? Why did you make James leave?" raising my brows.

"Well, your catheter needs changing and you need a sponge-bath."

I glanced at the clock on the wall. "At 9:30 in the evening! Man, I must smell bad and..."

She put her finger on my mouth. "It's not that silly. Most of the nurses on this floor are male. Your father didn't want any of them giving you a sponge bath, especially when you were in a coma. So, I offered to do it every day with a female nurse. She only has night shifts, so that's the only time I can give you one. I also use your favorite shower gel, not that antiseptic smelling hospital crap. James routinely leaves around that time so..." She shrugged making a point.

"Oh." I nodded my head in embarrassment.

Serenity got me a mirror from her bag of goodies. I looked at myself and wondered why the heck I looked better in a coma than on my regular days. The female nurse came in. She smiled and introduced herself as Nurse Liz. Serenity closed the curtains in my room. Nurse Liz removed the sheets covering me. There I saw this massive piece of gauze covering my stomach. There was a jumbo red dot and I noticed that my legs were hairless. "Seriously?" I peeked from under the sheets and glared at Serenity.

Nurse Liz snorted. "Your friend here has taken excellent care of you. You're lucky to have her, Miss Deuce."

"I know, but who's going to see my legs?"

Serenity jumped in to make a point. "Well, the idea is that you don't know and I'd rather be prepared. Maybe a hot nurse or doctor had to check your legs; I mean, imagine the horror of having hairy legs!"

"I was in a coma!" I rolled my eyes.

"Besides, the new employee is superb. And I could use the time off; so, there you were in a coma not able to argue with me, and I experimented with you. It was like having a real life-sized Barbie doll." She batted her lashes.

"Remind me to call Mattel and put in an order for Undertaker Barbie. Ha!" She and Nurse Liz both laughed.

An hour later, Nurse Paul came in and injected my IV bag with some meds. Nurse Liz was doing some rounds and Serenity opened the curtains. He made her go home since he had injected my IV with a sedative so I'd be able to sleep. I wasn't allowed to eat till tomorrow, and I was already wiped out. I didn't see her leave because I'd already given in to the painkillers.

7

I was never a morning person. But I was happy to see my sister that morning. She got me a bagel with herbal cream cheese. She and Julia were hitting it off. Everything had worked out for the best. Julia was in between jobs and my sister happened to hire her. They didn't stay very long because they had a lot to do, more or less; Julia had a lot of chaos to undo.

There was a TV in my room and found the remote control on my right nightstand. I flipped through the channels till I found a documentary about Ted Bundy. Why did he have to ram things into women's cervixes? Couldn't he be like any regular serial killer/rapist and torture them the old-fashioned way?

Michael and Clarabel had come in, hence cutting off my chain of sick theories. They weren't holding hands as they normally did. I remembered that Michael told me they were on a break; maybe they still were.

"You look good. How do you feel? Could you hear us talking to you? Michael told me that you woke up last night. Although I thought he was home- good thing he was here when you first opened your eyes." She sounded so bitter as if I were taking her boyfriend from her. *Again, I was in a coma- you, Bulimic Bitch.* I mean, he's my friend and that's what friends do when their friends are comatose. I wished that she would just self- combust that Wicked Witch of The West.

I decided to take the high road where there was less traffic and less road rage. "I'm doing ok. Thanks for asking. Both of you didn't have to bother yourselves in coming especially when

Michael was just here last night."

"You're not bothering us. It's the least I could do for letting you go home by yourself. I had an inkling that you weren't leaving with Angelo. I'm so sorry. Can you ever forgive me?" he pleaded.

"Michael, I decided to go home by myself because I just felt like being alone. So, stop beating yourself. I was at the wrong place at the wrong time -a once in a lifetime incident, how the heck would either of us have known something like that was going to happen? Besides, there's nothing to forgive you for so stop badgering me." *I had enough of this shit. Back off.*

He was holding my hand and making circle movements on my palm with his index finger. Clarabel huffed: "Michael, she's ok now. Like she said, stop beating yourself up. Come to think of it, she probably would've fallen off that motorcycle with you that day. The roads were so slippery, and you were driving like a madman."

I opened my eyes in horror and glared at Michael's direction. "What the hell? Is Jessy ok? Are you ok?" I did a once-over.

"Yeah, I'm ok. Just a few bruises and scratches; Jessy on the other hand needs some fixing. She got beat up pretty badly."

"Don't worry, once I'm on my feet we'll fix her. We'll go to the junkyard and get her some parts, then we'll take her to Darwin's; he'll fix her up. Don't worry about the prices, he owes me big."

He smiled at me as if someone granted him one of his three wishes.

"Michael, when will you ever learn that motorcycles are dangerous? You're going to spend a lot of money to fix it this time. Someday, you'll end your career as a professional dancer because of an accident. If it were someone else like your childhood friend here, it wouldn't matter that much. She doesn't make a living using her legs like you and I do." She crossed her arms across her two mosquito bites.

Michael opened his mouth in fury. "How could you-...." I cut him off before he got angry and started an argument with her. I put up my weak hand motioning Michael to shut up. I took a deep breath and shifted my body towards her.

"Listen, umm, Clarabel. If you've noticed, I just got out of a coma and it's only 10 in the morning so I'm not at all in the mood for this." She rolled her eyes at me. I continued.

"I don't know how your parents raised you, but it is rude to roll your eyes at someone." Too bad I couldn't physically jump out of my bed and put her in a chokehold. I digress.

"The snide comments and shitty assumptions need to stop. I do use my legs to make a living because without them I can't dig, you see. And the motorcycle is a "she" not an "it" and her name is Jessy. She's been with Michael for 10 years and I've known him ever since we were in diapers. So, don't think for one second you can address my friend this way in front of me. Show a little respect for him. He loves you and you're just being a bitch." It was like a ton of bricks lifted off my chest.

"Michael, how can you allow her to talk to me like this?" He didn't budge. She then turned to me. "You're a freak, Undertaker. If you gave a damn about his career, you would've been a good friend and not let him ride that motorcycle. Oh, and by the way, he doesn't love you so stop spending time with him. Only a slut would ride on the back of a motorcycle with someone else's boyfriend around town." Michael stiffened next to me I held his hand down. He had never heard her say such things. It's a good thing he was sitting next to me. Michael's angry teenage-self wanted to come out to play. She was undoubtedly provoking him.

I straightened myself. "Listen, Tampax. I'm surprised that his dick never fell off from engaging in coitus with what your vagina appears to be; a tub of acid. Now take your filthy ass and leave my room. If I ever see you here or on my street, I'll make sure to bury you myself- alive." Nurse Paul had heard the commotion and called security. They 'escorted' her out. Paul winked at me. It seems she wasn't in his cup of coffee either. Michael was still sitting next to me and hadn't moved. I could not fathom the idea of him or her any longer. First, he brings her to my mother's funeral, and he didn't even approach me for condolences because of her; now he brings her to my hospital room where she clearly shouldn't be. *I'm going to fix this.*

"Michael, I'm so sorry I don't want you to end your career. But I can't make you choose between me and her. You love her but I can't stand a bitch like her being disrespectful to me or my family. I've known you to have always been a very strong person, but it seems you check your nuts at the door when you're with her. I hate to say this, but I can't be friends with you anymore. This is too hard- your girlfriend is royally pissed at the fact that you come visit me in a coma that just means that she has trust issues. Don't tell me that you guys are on a break because you're obviously not anymore. Yes, I was avoiding you that day because what you did was wrong, and you were denying it. I'm not a home wrecker so don't wreck mine with that bitch. The staff on this floor don't even like her because she's rude. They have asked me like 8 times ever since I woke up if I wanted her banned. I said it was okay. I've put up with her for too long for you and I'm in no way obligated to continue."

Michael froze. He couldn't talk and I couldn't tell if he was breathing. He finally managed to utter: "I never knew that you felt this way about her. Why didn't you tell me? We've never kept secrets from each other. I'm not mad about your little scuffle with her but I'm mad about the fact that you've felt this strong about her that you've decided to keep those feelings to yourself. What's worse is that you tell me that you can't be friends with me anymore because of her. You understand I can't let that happen. We're family." His eyes were tearing up. *Really Michael? Did it not register?* The guy must have no emotional IQ.

"You can't have the best of both worlds. You've been with her for almost four years and I assume that you want to marry her someday. Let's face it she's never liked me and I'm alright with that. But when she says stuff like that in front of me, that's where I draw the line. I imagine that she's very nice when the two of you are together and that she makes you happy. She wants the best for you. On a higher note, I want you to take that jacket from my house and give it to her. You shouldn't be giving your female friends such lavish presents. It's inappropriate. I think Clarabel knows about the jacket that's why she's in her 'normal' mood than usual. This has to stop."

It was already starting to feel like a telenovela. My inner voice was rolling her eyes in Spanish.

"Please don't do this to me. There's no one like you who I can talk to. You're the only one who understands and accepts me for who I am. I can't stand to lose you again. You don't have to do this to us. Who's going to go on long rides in the rain with me? Who's going to make sarcastic comments about my ballet shoes? Who's going to sit front row on opening night just to watch me after flying eight straight hours, jetlagged? No one does that but you." His lips quivered.

"That's what friends do. But things are different now. I don't want this to turn into a Greek tragedy and I absolutely need you to not make this hard on me than it already is. This is for your own good. I don't want us to end up hating each other."

"Are you kidding me? Are you trying to hurt me? Because if you are, you're doing one heck of a job. I don't need this. I'm staying away from you if that's what you wish. I'm leaving in two weeks to Prague. I must prepare for opening night. You don't have to come. I'll reimburse you for plane ticket you booked three months ago. You know what? I don't want you to come. I can't believe you'd say such a thing to me. I can't believe you made such a big deal over a jacket. If you hadn't been so stubborn that day, I wouldn't have fucked up Jessy and you wouldn't have been shot. This is all because you thought I had some high school boy crush on you. It was just a token of my appreciation for all the times you traveled half around the world to always watch me on opening night. That's all there was to it, just a fucking thanks for all the times you went out of your way for me. For all the times I made you watch me countless hours as I tried to perfect dance moves. For all the times that you were there for me during my darkest hours. For all of the times you ditched your dates on prom night so that I wouldn't be alone cause no one wanted to date the ballerina with balls." He took a deep breath and started yelling more.

"For all the times you snuck money into my wallet when I was low on cash and too proud to ask. For all the times you cleaned up my vomit when I got pissed drunk over some girl who dumped me. For all the times you encouraged me to pursue my passion when no one else did. For all the times you tolerated Clarabel when I knew she wasn't nice to you. or all the times you never complained about anything and for all the times you loved me no matter how difficult I was."

I answered laboriously: "That's what families and friends do you, moron."

He threw his hands in the air. "Family and friends draw the line at many things but you are the most selfless person I've ever met but now, you're being the most selfish. I'm the one who never wants to see you again. You've abandoned me. Have a nice hell."

He stormed out of the room and there was that steel lump in my throat. I couldn't bring myself to cry. That was the worst feeling ever and I didn't know how my dad did it. I just remembered that I didn't see my father cry at my mother's funeral. That must've been a bitch. I suddenly realized that my father hadn't come in to visit me yet.

Nurse Paul's shift was almost over, and he was just doing some last-minute changes with my accessories. I asked him about my father, and he told me that he was running a bit late because he had to stop at work before he came over. He also told me that he had an investigator come with him to ask me a few questions for procedural purposes.

Whatever the hell that meant...

"Your friend doesn't realize how much he loves you. But you don't return these feelings. He doesn't love that girl, he thinks that he does." Nurse Paul was trying to make a point.

"I don't love him that way and neither does he. He loves that girl but they're just going through a rough patch - that's all. He's just used to me being around." I explained.

Nurse Paul grinned sarcastically: "Sweetheart, Dementia can be such a bitch."

8

Where was my dad when I needed him? It was already 12 p.m. and no sign of his presence. And where was Serenity when I needed her? I knew that she wouldn't come before 5 but still. I was edgy and agitated. I had had too much drama for one day and I didn't like it. That was like absorbing six months of PMS in one day.

One of the nurses brought in lunch. I've never tasted hospital food even when I was hospitalized, but I'd smelt it a few times and it wasn't good. I tried not to inhale as to not make a face. I was feeling a bit nauseated and didn't want to throw up. I did not want any surprises. I also didn't want to be disrespectful.

"You're going to have to eat lunch. We're going to try and get you out of bed today to take a few steps. Don't worry, it's not hospital food." She winked at me. I inhaled. "Your dad passed by and dropped it off for you. I emptied the food from their containers and put it in the hospital's plastic canisters and serving dish. Your father has expensive taste, Miss Deuce. He'll be here in half an hour."

"Umm...thanks nurse." She placed the tray on a high table for eating and propped up my back very slowly. My body was so sore. When she made sure all was well, she excused herself and left.

I removed the lid from the canister dish. My dad had ordered lobster for me with a side of grilled vegetables. It was my favorite dish when I was a child. There were also curly fries and steak sauce. I speared a piece of lobster and shoved it into my mouth.

Oh, Dear God- how I've missed food. I dipped a curly fry in the steak sauce, and it was dreamy and creamy. My palates were getting a good workout.

"Hey kiddo!" My father had arrived.

"Daddy!" I said.

"How's the grub? Now take it easy on yourself, alright?"

"Grub? This is anything but grub. It's amazing! Thanks, Dad. By the way, the nurse told me that you're bringing in someone from the precinct to question me. Something about procedure. I can't seem to remember."

"Yes, that's true. He's on his way up. He's Lieutenant Prique. He has some questions to ask and some things to explain to you. He's interrogated everyone, including your sister and me. I have also arranged for a lawyer to be present, just in case this needs to go to court."

"Lawyer? Court? Am I in trouble or something? I'm the one who got shot, remember? Don't tell me that guy who shot me is still alive and pressing charges against me!"

"No, no Sweetie. We are the ones suing. I got you the best lawyer in town. The guy who shot you is still alive. But I'm not allowed to reveal anything to you till Lieutenant Prique arrives."

"Alright, whatever." I exhaled. I continued enjoying my food and my father was fidgeting the whole time. He never fidgets. Something's not right. I chose not to ask any more questions.

There he was, Lieutenant Prique, a well-dressed man I might say. He was wearing cufflinks with a crisp white shirt. I was almost blinded by his shiny shoes. He had the smoothest shave and short sideburns. He was probably in his mid-forties but didn't look older than 35.

He walked up to me and introduced himself. "Miss Deuce, I'm Lieutenant Francis Prique. I'll be working on your case. Are you up to answering questions? Your father and I got the green light from Dr.York. He told us that you were quite responsive, but we shouldn't pressure or overwhelm you."

"Lieutenant Prique, I will answer anything you want but you tell me what's going on."

"Miss Deuce, how about if I ask you the questions and after that I explain to you what's going on? Would that be with you? It's how we do things."

"Sure, no problem."

"Miss Deuce, do you usually commute by bus?"

"No, I don't. I routinely use my car."

"Do you remember the day that you were shot?"

"Yes, I do."

"Can you tell me what the weather was like and who you saw before you got on the bus?"

"It started to drizzle a bit when I left work. I was waiting for my father outside because he had told me he would pick me up. Instead, I found Michael Nabakov waiting for me outside. Dad had sent him to pick me up because he was held up at the precinct. I refused to go with Michael and wound up going to the bus stop. It started to rain heavily. The bus arrived in two minutes. I got on the bus and it rained some more. I remember wringing my hair."

"Miss Deuce, why did you refuse to go with Mr. Nabakov?"

"We were having some differences and I didn't want to be around him. It was my first day back at work after my mom's funeral."

"What types of differences?"

"Lieutenant, with all due respect to you and the police force, my differences with my friend has nothing to do with the case. Michael Nabakov didn't shoot me, a crazed guy did. And by the way, the only thing I can remember about my shooter is that he had green eyes, Michael has hazel eyes." I raised my eyebrows proudly.

"Miss Deuce, it's my job to ask you these questions. They may seem unrelated to you but not to the investigation. Please let me do my job." My father was not happy with me talking to the lieutenant that way. I was taught to always respect the police no matter what they asked. He was glaring at me. I ignored him.

"Alright and I'm going to practice my right to an attorney." I looked at my dad.

"Miss Deuce, you do not need an attorney. You are not being accused of anything. I need to ask you these questions for they are pertinent to the case. I know the ordeal that you have been subjected to is not an easy one. I understand that you are scared and physically *and* emotionally drained. I really do. Please do not take my questions personally. I need to do my job so that justice is served." He was very calm and composed. I calmed down a bit. What crawled up my derriere?

"I am sorry, Lieutenant Prique. I... just feel..." He cut me off mid-sentence.

"I understand." He laid a warm hand on mine.

"The lawyer's waiting outside. Let me call him." My father chided.

My father re-entered the room with what seemed like a dead ringer of Ron Perlman. He was very much a look-alike. My mom told me that he used to be a double for the real Mr. Perlman and that's how he paid his way through law school. He turned to Lieutenant Prique and shook hands with him.

"I'm Vincent Kramer, the Deuces' family attorney and I'll be representing Miss Polly Deuce. If you would excuse us, Lieutenant Prique, I'd like a few minutes with my client. I know that you are Mr. Deuce's friend, but I cannot let his daughter answer any questions on record till she's spoken to me due to the sensitivity of the case."

What in the fabric softener fresh hell was this?

The Lieutenant seemed a bit miffed but then his expression turned into a half smile. "Alright, Vincent. You can talk to Polly I'll be in the cafeteria getting coffee for all of us. I'll have to bring my partner in, since this is turning official. Two sugars, right?"

"Yes, brown sugar. I won't take long Francis. Johnny, if you don't mind, I need to have the room to myself so that I can talk to your daughter."

"Sure, whatever you need Vince. Got to go anyways. See you Wednesday night. James plans on kicking your ass this time, Hellboy."

They high-fived each other like a bunch of college kids. My father left and I was all alone with Mr. Kramer wondering what the heck was going on.

"Polly?"

"Yes, Mr. Kramer?"

"Please, call me Vince. Listen Polly, your mom, rest in peace, was like a sister to me. So, don't worry about anything. Francis is just doing his job and he's a great guy. They have the shooter, but the situation is complicated. Francis just wants to eliminate some factors, that's all. Don't take it too personal. Don't answer any questions we haven't discussed without me. He knows that Michael didn't take you home that day and that he claims to have been in a motorcycle accident. He just wants to hear your side of the story. The situation is that Michael may be a suspect and Francis needs to get all his facts straight."

Huh?

"Michael? A suspect? My Michael, twinkle-toes-motorcycle-riding-jazz-fingers Michael? Are you crazy? Is Lieutenant fucking Prique nuts or something? Michael would rather be a quadriplegic than hurt me!"

"I see that. Who are your two best friends?"

"Serenity and Michael. Well, Michael not even a friend anymore."

"Not the point. They did a background check on Serenity and she's clean. Michael not so much."

"Yeah, I know that. My father used to bail him out when he got into fights. He went through a rough patch when he was 16. I mean, he was a teenager with no father."

"Yeah, but Michael never told you how his father died?"

"Yes, he did. His father was involved with very bad people. Something to do with the Russian mob. His mother never hid that fact from him. She told him this when he was twelve. I mean Michael is Russian and his mother is from Pennsylvania."

I had no idea why I added that last bit of information.

"That's very true. It is believed that Michael was recruited by the same people who killed his father. How do you think he got the money to help his mother with her mortgage?"

"He's a professional ballet dancer for Christ's sake! He is the lead dancer in his own show, and they've been touring for many months and I've been to each one of those opening nights in every country He has been a professional dancer for over 15 years It's his livelihood. Don't give me that crap. Michael is the sweetest guy ever and I will not have you giving me false facts about him."

"Polly, Sweetheart. They've been tracking Michael's every move for almost a year. His girlfriend's father is a mobster and he has helped Michael and his mother a lot. Julia is in the dark."

"Isn't Clarabel Russian as well?" I was slow today.

"Half- Half. Her mother is Ukrainian, but her father is Russian."

In my mind, it was the same. USSR, anyone?

All this new info had my head spinning. I couldn't help but start laughing. Was I on someone's hit list?

"So, you're meaning to tell me that Michael conspired a fusillade to kill me?" I couldn't stop giggling.

"No, I wish it were that simple."

"Then please enlighten me I'm losing my patience." Giggles had subsided.

"If you recall there were four hostiles. One of those hostiles was an undercover FBI agent. Another was believed to be Michael and the other two were his accomplices."

"Huh? How can that be? Believed to be Michael? I don't understand."

"One hostile who was the driver was shot. Another was captured and one ran away but..." I cut him off mid-sentence.

"You mean to tell me that Michael was the one who shot me? That's why he wrapped his arms around me. Oh My God! But wait, my shooter had green eyes!"

"No, the one that ran away is believed to be Michael and your shooter is an undercover FBI agent. He was going to shoot

Michael so that he wouldn't leave the bus. Your back was facing the boys and you thought that the agent wanted to shoot them. You didn't know that there was a hostile trying to jump out the moving bus. You got in the way and the gun went off by accident. Now, this is the agent's statement. He's in custody now. I'm here to help you sue the FBI agent who almost killed you. Francis Prique is trying to get your statement and he's also trying to put together the timeline between you seeing Michael and the bus incident."

I started feeling queasy. Just remembering that day made me shudder. But then I remembered something.

"Vince, the FBI agent shot two people behind me in cold blood. They had a duffle bag."

"Polly, Honey. Those two people behind you were terrorists and there was a bomb in that duffle bag. If he hadn't shot them, they would have detonated it; killing hundreds of people in a ten-mile radius."

"But, umm--I can't seem to wrap my head around this. Michael couldn't have had the time to go to the bus. Ugh! What do I know?"

"Look, Michael trashed his own motorcycle. He was doing a job for Clarabel's father and failed. Michael is not who you think. His motorcycle accident isn't consistent with his injuries. He doesn't know that the FBI is onto him. He's using his dancing career as a cover-up. Please understand what I'm telling you. I'm here to defend you and it's not in my interest to tell you lies. I'm here to help you sue the agent and Michael. Your father's friends at the FBI are talking to your sister right now."

"This is too much for me. I need to think this over. I can't do this now. Too much info. Can I not answer any of Prique's questions?"

"You don't have to. I'll take care of it. Just rest for now and

I'm going to send your father, okay?"

"Does he know any of this?"

"Yes, of course he does." He winked at me.

Ron Perlman left the room and I was trying to take in my newfound info - my newfound world of lies. My father came in and sat next to me. We had a very silent conversation, yet the longest one we've ever had. He then held my hand and asked me: "Polly, can I tell you something? This is my opinion and don't take this the wrong way, alright?"

"Dad, I don't think that I can take anything the wrong way now, cause all of it is wrong in every way possible." I was resting my head on his chest. I felt very tired.

"Don't let anyone, Francis, Vince or me for the matter, tell you what to do. Don't hear things through the grapevine but hear them from the horse's mouth."

"Are you saying they are lying to me?"

"No, baby. Of course not. I was referring to the FBI agent. " He somewhat postulated.

9

I woke up around 3 p.m. feeling overwhelmed. Since there was no one in the room, I took the liberty of crying my eyes out till I felt better. I had too many emotions bottled up. I felt betrayed, hurt and most of all –scared. How could the Michael I knew once, be a villain? The boy I grew up with eating Gummy bears. The boy who always came to my "Valentine's Day Blows" parties – with his date. The boy who always let me put make-up on him just to cheer me up when I was sad. The boy who practiced numberless hours of pas de bourrées and somersaults. The boy who waited for me on opening nights. The boy who would never hurt me. The boy who once beat a guy for making fun of my love handles. The boy who once took me on rides on his bike. The boy who bought me a ten-hundred-dollar jacket. The boy whom I hurt this morning. The boy who I knew now was trying to hurt many people. Boy, oh boy! That's how he got the money...

Walking three steps around was easy that day. My intense physical therapy, which lasted four weeks, was strenuous and painful- *sort of*. No amount of medication could numb the fear that I had. I was afraid and I didn't know why. I hadn't seen Michael again since the last time I saw him. He must be in Prague now. I wanted to go on opening night, but my father advised against it, although the doctors cleared me for traveling with an escort. Serenity had offered to travel with me. I hadn't had the chance to tell her anything. I didn't have a moment of solitude ever since I left the hospital three weeks ago.

I missed work. I missed Uncle James, Marc and Angelo. I missed my job and my life. I missed my mom. It started to hit me slowly that she was gone. I had no one to turn to for advice. I demanded from Vince to set up a meeting with my MP3 snatcher, who was in prison. I needed to see this person to have closure. I didn't want to put a guy who served his country in jail just because he almost killed me. *Yeah, I know. I am twisted that way. I am also curious to hear this guy out.*

Vince didn't need to pull that many strings. My dad was a forensic artist and many people owed Uncle James.

"Are you sure it's wise to do this?" My sister asked me as she was pouring me a cup of coffee.

"Anne, for the millionth time, I need closure. I mean, I need to see whom I'm pressing charges against. I need to materialize my shooter in my head. I need perspective." *You'd think I was writing a dissertation from the last description.*

"Polly, didn't you get your perspective from the bomb you dropped on Serenity yesterday? You're lucky she's still talking to you. But I do give you credit for trying to meet the guy before you press charges against him."

I decided to ignore Anne that morning, she was being very pushy and talkative- *so not like her*. "Dad, can we go now, please?"

"Okay, let me walk you to the car."

"No, I want to do it by myself today. I haven't left the house in three weeks and the physical therapist said that I need to start depending on myself. By the way, I need to schedule with her this week. I want to start going to the clinic. Physical therapy at home sucks."

"You're welcome. Okay, just be careful." *My dad, always the wisenheimer.*

I got up by myself and walked slowly to the back door that lead to our driveway. It was painful – not the walking but the memory of Michael waiting there for me on summer mornings with Jessy. I slowly reached my father's car and sat down in the passenger's seat next to the driver. I remembered the last time I was here, I had had a fight with Michael over that damn jacket. I left him devastated that day and could still see his sad image in the

visor.
My dad started the car and inserted a CD. "Who's this?"
"Well, Polly. This is a band that I'm playing with."
I made a mental note of finishing a sentence with a preposition.
"But, it's rock. You don't play rock music. You play the cello for Pete's sake."
"Yeah I know. I play guitar bass here."
"You never played the bass." Great, now my father was also keeping secrets from me.
"It's almost the same concept. I had been practicing for a year. I've kind of mastered it now."
"You sound great."

We reached the FBI headquarters. Vince had told us to meet him there because they were transferring my MP3 snatcher there. Two agents escorted us inside. I was only allowed to enter the investigation room with Vince. My father decided to leave for work at the precinct. The halls were well-lit and very clean. We entered an investigation room and it was cold in there. Vince gave me his jacket to wear. I had been very sensitive to cold ever since I got shot. Maybe I should sue for body heat. We sat at an oval table made of Formica with a slab of glass in the middle. An agent entered the room and went directly to Vince. He whispered something in Vince's ear. Vince put his hand on my hand showing me support. I didn't bother to ask him what that was about.
After five tantalizing minutes, two agents brought in my shooter in handcuffs. They sat him down in front of me; two agents on his left and one lawyer-looking dude on his right *or maybe his union rep?* I just stared at my MP3 snatcher. Vince squeezed my shoulder. The lawyer-looking dude put his hand out and introduced himself.
"Hi, Miss Deuce, Mr. Kramer, I'm Eddie Ball and I'll be representing Mr. Black. We really appreciate that you're meeting Mr. Black before pressing charges against him."
"Mr. Ball, Miss Deuce had intended for this meeting to happen

sooner if it weren't for her life-threatening injuries and weeks of physical therapy. She was in an induced coma for almost a week because of your client's carelessness. He's an FBI agent and managed to pull the trigger 'by accident' hence, shooting Miss Deuce at close range. This resulted in a through and through not to forget, Miss Deuce still has some trouble breathing and may not be able to go back to work for a while." It was funny how Vince sounded all lawyer-y.

"Mr. Kramer, you are very much aware of the situation here; it was a matter of life or death. My client takes full responsibility and is willing to pay Miss Deuce her hospital bills and a settlement for her time off work."

I was surprised he didn't throw the terms 'collateral damage' around.

"Monetary compensation and jail time." Vince growled.

I hadn't looked straight at my shooter's direction ever since he came in. I managed to look up at him while Eddie and Vince were at each other's throats. I was scared but then I remembered how he wrapped his arms around me and how he whispered in my ear. I pulled myself together and managed to look his way. There, they were those green eyes that glowed like two massive emeralds. His hair was pulled back to his nape in a pony tail. Eddie and Vince's lawyer bitching had become white noise. I couldn't help myself but be fond of Mr. Black's facial features. He was striking and – those lips, God's a great plastic surgeon. Something seemed familiar about him though. Vince tugged me.

"Miss Deuce, how would you like to proceed with the points I mentioned to Mr. Ball?"

I made believe that I had been listening. "I'm not happy with any of the proceedings."

Ummm...what?

Vince looked mortified. I asked Mr. Ball if I could address his client personally. He gave me the okay.

Mr. Black couldn't have looked more than twenty-five to me. He looked quite young to be an agent. I was told earlier that he was thirty-three. He glanced my way and finally spoke: "Miss Deuce, I didn't mean for all of this to happen. I take full responsibility. I had to shoot those two people behind you; they were terrorists and they had a bomb. You got in the way more than once which is understandable."

"Mr. Black, I'm aware of this. My attorney has explained this situation to me. I just want to know if it's true what they say about Michael Nabakov." Eddie shifted his body to the imprisoned agent's side and told him he didn't have to answer my question. He shushed Eddie.

"Michael, whom I've learned is your best friend, was involved with the big boss who recruited me. He's talked to me a lot about you and how he never actually loved Clarabel. Miss Deuce, Michael Nabakov worked sometimes for Clarabel's father delivering packages. He didn't know what he was getting himself into till it was too late. Still, Michael is facing much more serious charges than I am. He's an accessory to murder. He will also be charged with aiding and abetting."

"I can't believe what I'm hearing. Accessory to murder? If he's all these things, how come you guys haven't arrested him yet?"

One of the agents who hadn't moved, approached me. "We were hoping that you would help us out. That's why we scheduled this meeting."

"I know where this is going and 'no' I will not help you." I stood up. "Mr. Black, I'm not pressing any charges against you on one condition that you don't touch Michael Nabakov. There must be a good explanation for all this. I think he was under duress. Moreover, if you knew me, why the fuck did you shoot me you son of a bitch!?"

"I said that he talked to me a lot about you, but I never knew what you looked like. He never gave away whether you lived in the US or Russia. I didn't even know your name. He was very careful about not revealing your identity. I did not press him. Miss Deuce, I've been undercover for a year with Mr. Nabakov. I am sure he was once a good guy but he's voluntarily doing these things for a cause. He is convinced that Americans killed his

father. Mr. Nabakov will have to face the consequences."
"Then, I'm sorry, I'm not dropping any charges against you. I hope you rot in prison. I am loyal to my friend no matter what, he needs help and I will never believe that he's this type of person. And you owe me an MP3 player you, dickwad!" Vince and I got up and just left the room.

"Polly, I'll do everything in my power to put Mr. Black away. You didn't have to drop charges against him in the first place. It is rumored that he became a rogue agent and they are hiding it."
Why are most good-looking guys asses? Summabitch handsome stupid MP3 snatcher.

Vince drove me home. I messaged Serenity; I needed to talk to her.

`Hey girl, can u pass by after work? I need 2ttu. don't tell any1. Luv u,mwa!`

She texted me back.

`I was gonna pass by nws. I'm the 1 who needs 2ttu.c u l8er.`

Vince escorted me to the door and left. I walked to the living room and plopped myself on the couch in the living room. What's up with all the reruns? Ah, Mexican soap operas, the men always cry, and the women are promiscuous. I woke up an hour later feeling light-headed and no one was home. I went to the kitchen to get myself a glass of cold water. My lips had been always parched lately due to the meds I was taking. The door knocked and it was Serenity. *Thank God.* I offered her some tea and we sat in the kitchen talking all evening. I told her every detail about Michael, Clarabel, Vince and my shooter.

"Umm, Babe, what is your shooter's name by the way?"
"I forgot. His last name is Black though. The only thing I remember is that he had green eyes and was very good-looking. And he owes me an MP3 player. I can't believe what he told me about Michael and..." she cut me off.
"Did you say that you his last name is Black? Did he have reddish hair that was tied back? And he had sort of pouty lips and he is really pale?"

"Umm..yeah coming to think of it. He also looked kind of familiar to me."

"That's because you've met him, Silly. Oh my God! How could I have missed that?"
"Missed what? Stop torturing me."
"He's Sandy Black's brother!"
"Who the hell is Sandy Black? I don't know any girl by that name."
My brain was short-circuiting.

"Polly! The caterer from your mom's funeral, his name is Sandy Black and his brother, Castor, was the guy wearing the Ray Ban's you hated so much. You couldn't shut up about his hair and ass that day, remember?"
My inner voice's jaw dropped.

"What the hell? Since when do FBI agents cater at funerals? I'm confused."
"Castor Black helps out Sandy sometimes with the business when he's off duty or on vacation. Castor's an FBI agent!"
"What the hell? How do you know these things?"
"You were describing him to me before and I remembered your mom's funeral. Then, it all made sense! The same descriptions fit but you didn't see his eyes the first time. They live in my neighborhood. No wonder Sandy's been acting weird, it's because his brother is locked up for shooting you by accident!

Castor's a good client at my shop and that's why I haven't been seeing him! Polly, he's a good guy. I know these people well. Give Vince a call and ask him about your shooter's first name."

"What good is that going to do me, huh? You think that I'm going to drop charges against him. He wants to put Michael away, remember? Besides, I don't care."

"What do you mean you don't care? If the guy didn't feel guilty for shooting you, he wouldn't have hugged you- then and there. It's Michael and his bulimic whore who are bad news not Castor. Babe, you should drop the charges against him. You're feeling better now and he's going to do time anyways. He was protecting you. It's the only theory."

"Oh man, I think I'm going to give myself an aneurysm just thinking about this."

"Girl, trust me on this. Castor is a client at my bookshop. Look, he's into those books about vampires, ghosts and all mystical creatures. He even gave me the brand of conditioner he uses for his hair."

"Yes, his hair. I remember now, it falls to the small of his back. Isn't that like against FBI decorum or something?"

"Well, he told me he's a field agent and his look, helps him in many undercover situations. No wonder he was able to fit in with Michael's mob."

"Michael's mob." I echoed silently...

Yesterday, he was a ballerina, today he's Michael the Mobster. He's been missing for a few days. Despite everything, I hope he's ok.

Here came that sunken feeling again.

Serenity left my home that evening and I went upstairs. I got into bed without even brushing my teeth. I couldn't help it, but I couldn't stop thinking about my mystery shooter. Castor Black was trying to shoot Michael and I got in the way. Castor Black was the cute caterer guy at my mom's funeral. Castor Black was going to lock Michael away. I didn't know Greek gods could multi-task and I didn't know that ballerinas could join the mob.

10

I was never a morning person. Serenity had offered to drive me on Saturday mornings to the clinic for my physical therapy sessions. It was a thirty-minute drive and it always felt like more than that. I was having trouble sitting in one place for too long. We stopped by a McDonald's drive through for some breakfast. We rarely ate Mc Donald's.

"I'm going to order you a Big Mac."

"Thanks, Babe."

"Did you call Vince?"

"No, I went straight to bed last night and barely made it downstairs this morning."

"Here's my phone. Call him. I'm dying here."

She handed me her phone. I could never work a touch screen. I was probably still the only person who owned a Blackberry. My father had purchased a touch screen for me. It was still in the box. There was a picture of me and Serenity on her phone's wallpaper. It was a very nice picture. We took it back when we were at a Halloween party last year. She was Lady Macbeth and I went as myself, and Michael as a female ballerina. *Where the hell was, he?*

"Hello?" A low voice answered.

"Hi, may I speak to Vince please?"

"Speaking."

"Vince, it's Polly. Is this a bad time?"

"Oh, no Sweetie. I'm at the office and I'm with clients. How can I help you? Do you need anything?"

"Yes, can you give me Mr. Black's first name and some

basic info about him?"

"Of course, one sec, I have the file here on my desk." I could hear him going through papers, it was nerve-wracking. *Three eye-rolling minutes later.*

"Polly? You still there?"

"Yes, you found the file?"

"Yeah, his name is Castor Black."

"Is his brother Sandy Black, of Salt and Pepper Catering?"

"Yes, actually. How do you know this?"

"*Serenity*." Making her name sound like an explanation.

"I don't understand."

"She's my best friend who used to be a paralegal. She lives on the same street as Castor and Sandy. I was telling her what happened with me. She was the one who put the pieces together. She owns a vintage book store and knows everyone."

"Aha, interesting. Then we need to meet up. Tell Serenity if she ever needs a job, my firm is open to her. We can use a paralegal like her here." I could hear him smiling over the phone.

"Yeah, umm, Vince, that will never happen. I've got to go now."

"I'll schedule a meeting with you later. Bye."

Serenity wasn't surprised when I told her about Castor Black. She gave me the 'I told you so' look. I hated that look.

"What's up? What are you laughing at?"

"I was just remembering how you got back at your bully boss. You drove that rich bitch crazy one day in front of her associates on purpose. The woman lost it. Remember?"

"Of course, I do, she tried to run me over the same day by 'accident'. I sued her for psychological damage and attempted murder. Girl, when a senior partner was representing me, he wiped that bitch clean. That woman put me through hell all those years. She was such a sociopath. Only till before that incident did the firm see her true colors."

"Didn't she get disbarred?"

"Of course, she did. I'm the rich bitch now with a bookshop and she's just a poor whore wearing an orange jumpsuit. Bet she's still wondering what just happened to her."

"I'm so happy you don't have to work for people like that anymore."

"Yeah, me too. I always promise myself to never treat any employee at the shop like that. I couldn't even if I tried. You have to be a special kind of crazy."

We reached the clinic and met up with my physical therapist. Serenity always sat on the side and encouraged me as if she were cheering her favorite basketball team. She also bribed me with Twinkies just to keep me moving and my therapist was none the happier. I needed to go to the bathroom badly, I mean two cups of coffee, a bottle of water and an energy drink had to go somewhere eventually. I told Serenity to wait for me till I went and took a very long leak.

The bathroom at the clinic was always very clean. After relieving myself on a pristine porcelain throne, I felt much better and lighter. I never liked using the hand dryer because hand dryers attracted all germs from around the bathroom and stuck them to your hands. Think of having a septic tank condensate in a box and blow hot air out of it. Paper towels were always a better option and if I didn't find any, I'd use my faithful jeans. I was looking into the mirror and I wasn't looking too shabby. It then hit me, I was wearing a tweed jacket- Michael's tweed jacket. He had bought it once as a joke when he was tutoring me in high school. I hated space geometry and still do. He used to wear it with eye glasses to sound professor-like. Then I'd wear it to tutor him in physics and chemistry. It was too big for both of us. I had my mother take it in when I worked at my last job. She also had sewn little skulls and a mini-triquetra on the lapels. It was my favorite jacket. I washed my face and looked into the mirror again and- one of the bathroom stall doors opened. It happened too fast, but someone grabbed me and covered my mouth and dragged me to the same stall. I didn't know whether to scream or defend myself. I froze.

He placed his finger on my lips. He removed his mask and held me against the stall wall. "Please, Polly. Don't scream." He pleaded.

I smacked his hands away.

"Michael, what do you think you're doing? The FBI is searching for you. What mess have you gotten yourself into? How could you lie to me?" I said in a low voice.

"Polly, I couldn't tell you. How the heck was I supposed to know that you were going to catch the first evening bus at the stop? It was raining and I assumed that you were either going to actually carpool with Marc or take the second evening bus."

"So, you just thought that it was ok planting a bomb on a bus if I weren't on it? Get off me!"

"No, Polly. I'm doing this for a cause. That's why I need you to hear me out."

"I don't want to hear it."

He kept one hand on my shoulder, hunched over and closed the lid of the bathroom seat and sat me down. He kneeled on the floor and held both my hands. *Oh, great.* He was going to deliver a freakin' keynote speech lecture like the ones our parents used to give us. He looked up at me and whispered:

"I'm not going to beat around the bush so I will get straight to the point but first you have to know that I would never ever do anything to hurt you intentionally. I'm still the same person you know but it's just I've taken a different route in my life. You know my father died when I was three and my mother has managed to take care of me all this time with the help of your parents. But I can't be a performer forever. There's a shelf life to what I do. I don't want to live a mediocre life and have a mediocre family with mediocre friends. Clarabel's dad has taken me in as if I were his son. They fight for a cause and have many beliefs - I am Russian and Clarabel is half Russian/ Ukranian. As you know, Russians live mediocre lives here unless they are part of a group. They go to Russia and learn ballet and come back here and take our jobs. Ballet dancing is by nature mostly than by nurture. I have failed Clarabel's father with this operation and yes, it was a bomb and it was meant to go off. It was just to send a message to a few people. How the hell was I supposed to know that a rogue agent was working undercover with them for three years? I had just met him ten months before the incident."

I sighed and couldn't believe what I was hearing. "You know something Michael? I wish that that agent had killed me so I wouldn't have to hear this incessant crap. You have changed and I don't know you. I begged them not to go after you and I threatened to press charges against the agent because he wanted to go after you. Now, you just proved him right and me, wrong. You are a traitor to your country. That's right! You didn't grow up in Russia you cheap bottle of vodka! My family, who isn't Russian, took you in. We were raised together. You were the only person I had ever trusted and now you want to kill people just to send a message!"

It was hard yelling in a low voice. We stood up together and I delivered a knee, as hard as I could, in the groin and punched him in the face. I opened the stall door and he was on the floor gasping for air. I turned and told him: "I hope that you understood this message that you are dead to me and I never want to see you again. You'd better prance because I'm calling the cops to arrest their Bombing Ballerina. I can't trust you. I hope you die you, immoral imp."

I left the bathroom and Serenity was standing outside. "Polly, what took you so long? I thought you collapsed from all the work you did today. Who were you talking to inside? You look pale."

"Babe, I'm fine I just feel a bit constipated from the meds. Don't worry about me." I managed to squeeze in a smile between words.

"Alright, but who were you talking to and you sounded

pissed."

"No one. There are other people who use the bathroom inside."

"I don't believe you. You're a sucky liar."

As she was opening the bathroom door, I held her arm and told her to let it go. She pushed me gently aside and went in. I expected not to find him inside like they do in the movies. She saw someone jump out the bathroom window. I was behind her. She turned and walked to me.

"Polly, I have a feeling that that was Michael. And if that was him, I advise you to call the police. I know how you feel about him but honey, he's not good. They'll charge you with aiding and abetting to a terrorist."

"You're right. It's just I don't feel it's him anymore. He's involved with some very bad people. Can you please take me to the FBI field office and call Vince?" I was trying not to cry.

"Sure, but who do you want to see at the FBI field office?"

"Castor Black" I said dryly. He was no longer in jail and was on modified duty as I was told.

'Why? Might I ask?"

"I don't know Serenity. I haven't figured it all out yet. Just take me there please." I said nervously.

Serenity had called Vince and he agreed to meet us at the headquarters with Castor's rep, Eddie Ball. I didn't know if he were his attorney or a union rep. Do FBI agents have union reps? When we reached there, we were escorted inside by two agents to the same room. I first asked to see someone working on my case. Lieutenant York had entered the room. He was a good friend of my father. Dad helped him work many cases. I sat him down and told him what had happened to me at the clinic earlier today. He listened without interrupting me even once. He then laid back in his chair and his lips moved.

"Polly, we expected that he'd 'drop in' but not in such a public place like the clinic. I'm grateful that you did the right thing. But I don't understand why do you need to see Castor Black. He's on modified duty for the time being."

"Please, Michael told me with his own mouth that they are conspiring against the government or whatever. Serenity saw him leave the bathroom! Please don't do this to him!"

"Miss Deuce, I thought you wanted to press charges against Castor if he pursued Michael."

"That's true but I heard it from the horse's mouth!" *Damn you, Dad and your analogies!*

"Alright, calm down. We'll call Mr. Black in. He'll be here in a minute with his attorney who happens to be here with him. He cannot have conversations with you or anyone pertaining to this case without representation. It is for your good and his good. Your dad is upstairs by the way. We're trying to keep him off any cases related to your case. We do not want anything compromising this case, especially conflict of interest."

Why wasn't my Dad at the precinct?

"I understand. Don't have to tell him I'm here now. You can tell him when I leave."

"Polly, I know how annoyed you are with everything, just take it easy on yourself. We are all here to help you. I'm very proud that you came straight here to tell us. You are very brave."

Was he going to give me a cookie for my bravery?

For some reason, Lieutenant York's conversation didn't do me any good. I started wondering if there was an actual difference between a tombstone and a headstone. I started imagining the first cavemen and how they made the first tombstones in order to make sure that the evil spirits stayed underground. Now if I just were a cavewoman burying Clarabel, I'd probably need to bury her twenty feet under then pour crap from a wooly mammoth, then a layer of steel and then cement. That bitch needed a super boulder as a headstone then to top that I'd take a dump on her grave. Pffft! How dare he? *Stop reverie, come Castor and his ball.*

He was wearing a powder blue Oxford shirt, dark blue

jeans and brown Chelsea boots. He had that same musky rosy-whatever- you- want- to- call- it scent. Vince cleared his throat. "Eddie, Miss Deuce would like to settle this outside court. As you've been notified, Mr. Nabakov paid her a little unwanted visit. My client was shaken up and we have a witness who saw Mr. Nabakov flee the scene. Miss Deuce needs to put this behind her."

"Vince, your client said that she will not drop the charges if my client, who's an FBI agent, goes after Mr. Nabakov." Eddie was being smug.

"Eddie, things have changed now. Castor told Polly revealed shocking news about her childhood friend and they've known each other ever since they were in diapers. You were telling her about someone who was a brother to her and her sister, and a son-like figure to her parents. You were unveiling information about someone she took baths with as a toddler and camped outside the backyard. Polly has invested in her friendship with Mr. Nabakov as much as she's invested with her relationship with her own sister. He is as good as blood. His house is her house and her house is his house. You need to understand the history Michael and Polly have together. She trusted him blindly until he paid her a visit at the clinic. The FBI can't seem to catch him. She wants nothing to do with this anymore and she just wants to drop the charges against Castor."

"How can she drop charges against my client when she knows zilch about him? Huh, Vince? Why the change of heart? Leave your poker face for Friday nights." He raised one side of his lips.

"Polly's best friend, Serenity, revealed some info about Castor to us. He turned out to work with his brother, Sandy. Polly had met him before at her mother's funeral, but your client was wearing sunglasses and he looked like a girl at first to her. *You know hair and all.* That's not the point. Serenity made it clear to us that Castor is a good member of society and that he's just dedicated to his job. We are dealing with a Catch 22 here. Eddie, stop busting my chops. Let's settle this or are you afraid you'll be out of work?"

"I work with the DA you cretin. Ok, so what do you want from us exactly just to be clear? We have poker tonight and don't forget to bring the steaks."

Castor got up and interrupted them. He held out his hands as if he were an arbitrator between two lovers. "Listen, Eddie can you and Mr. Kramer step out for a second? I need to talk to Miss. Deuce off record."

"Castor, I don't think that's a good idea and in my professional..." Castor cut him off. "She's willing to drop charges against me and you are making it difficult. I'd like nothing but go back to regular duty and maybe, just maybe, go home and sleep in my bed. Please, Eddie?" He raised his eyebrows.

Was he sleeping in the office?

"Alright Castor. But you're taking a risk."

"I have no problem. I'm right behind you Eddie." Vince got up and followed the ball. I was left all alone in the room with me, myself and a Greek god.

He stared at me for a moment and nothing came out of his mouth. I didn't want to speak either. It was like a staring competition. I just got fed up after two minutes of blaring silence. As I walked from my seat he got up and blocked my way to the door.

"Miss Deuce, you can't leave the room till you hear what I need to say." He faintly smiled.

"I don't need to hear anything from you. I'm dropping the charges and that's that. I don't know why you sent our lawyers away. There's nothing further for you to tell me. Michael's a criminal and you were trying to save the day. I got in your way and screwed things up for you. You ended up on modified duty with the risk of losing your job. To top that, Michael's a fugitive and I ended up with a hole in my freakin chest. So, if you're going to just sit there and have a telepathic conversation with me then I don't have time for this. Now, move out of my way please, I want to go home." *I thought I was going to cry, must be PMS... mmm...no, not till another three weeks.*

He looked at me all apologetic and...upset. "Be as it may. I'm sorry and thank you." He moved out of my way and opened the door for me. Vince was already standing outside with two cups in his hand.

Vince handed me a cup of coffee. "That was very quick. So, tell me. What did he tell you?"

"Nothing actually."

"What do you mean *'nothing'*? He must've said something."

"Really nothing."

"You mean you just stared at each other then you left?"

"I always knew you were clairvoyant." I scoffed.

"Serenity is waiting for you downstairs. I'll give you a call to tell you what happens."

"Okay, waiting for your call."

I rushed downstairs as fast as I could. Serenity was checking out the wanted list. She was seeing which criminal was the hottest.

"Geez, why are all the hot ones the bad ones?"

"You're asking the wrong person."

"So, what happened?"

"Nothing and don't ask me what he said. We just stared at each other after he made the lawyers leave the room. He wanted to talk to me off the record." I rolled my eyes and explained what I told him in the end before exiting the room.

"You mean to tell me he just stared at you, then you left the room after giving him a rap on the knuckles?"

"Rap on the what? Girl, you read too much. And yes, it is like I said."

"I think he's mesmerized by you. What I don't understand is how he saw you at the funeral and didn't recognize you on the bus."

"Mesmerized? Again, less books more Cosmo. On another note, I think it's because I didn't have bangs at the time. You remember? We got bangs three days before I went back to work."

"Yeah...Well, I was trying to change your look and hey it worked like a charm!"

Yeah, it did. Fashion almost got me killed.

"Listen, I know things are crazy. But I have to drive you home now because I have to get back to the shop."

"Oh, I'm sorry. Let's go. I really need a long hot shower and a nap."

I had been a bit selfish today.

We were on our way out the headquarters and I saw Castor Black. He was on his way out as well. It seems that our lawyers did a good job and hopefully things were settled. Almost everyone I knew there had Wednesday nights at a different house playing poker with my dad and Uncle James. He stopped to talk to Serenity who was walking by my side.

"Hey, Serenity. How are you? Please keep my books on hold, I'll pick them up Monday morning. Sorry, couldn't come before as you've seen I had been caught up." He stared at me and I looked the other way.

"No, problem Castor. When Polly told me, what was really going on, I instantly knew it was you. So, they let you go? I mean is everything ok?"

"Yes, just now. They released me, but I have a hearing next month I think." He then turned to me. "Polly, again thank you for dropping the charges. If there's anything you need, Serenity has my number."

"Thank you but that won't be necessary. Have a nice day and if you need anything just have your lawyer call my lawyer."

I turned to Serenity. “Can we go please?” She hugged him goodbye and we left. I couldn’t believe it when I got to the car, I just needed to sit down. Serenity was smiling and driving like a cartoon high on butterflies and happiness. That was a seven on my barf-o-meter.

11

We reached the driveway of my house and Serenity asked me if she could come in for a glass of water. I bet all that smiling made her thirsty and hungry. We went into the kitchen and I made her a sandwich because I knew that she probably wouldn't be able to pass by the local Italian deli and get one. I didn't even bother to ask her if she was hungry. I knew she would refuse as to not trouble me. We have been friends for many years, but some things never change with her. I have learned to accept that this is who she is; selfless Serenity. She smiled as I handed her the sandwich.

"You like him, don't you?"

"What? Who?"

I didn't like perplexing questions.

"You like Castor, Polly. I know how you treat guys you like. You have this Modus Operandi. You get nervous and shut down. Then, you totally ignore him not leaving a sliver of hope for the poor sucker. It helps that you don't treat him like a cadaver at the parlor, you know. He has a pulse and everything. Also, you don't have to lay him to rest, he can do it all by himself." Her smile was turning creepy and for the first time I wanted to smack her. She'd beat the shit out of me, but I could try.

"I almost...*almost* chuckled. Very funny Serenity. I am glad to know that I have a Modus Operandi like, let's say, a serial killer! Where did you get the idea that I like him? He shot me. I can't go back to work for another few weeks." My resting bitch face would have put supermodels to shame.

"Yeah, that's the problem." She rolled her eyes. "You liked him ever since the first time you saw him. If he were my type, I would take him. I wouldn't mind getting shot by an Adonis."

"This conversation is so wrong on so many levels. Buttercup, there's nothing there. He's just weird. He just stares at me. It is the creepiest thing."

She went into her ultra-sonic mimicking mode. "He shot me. Bla bla. He's weird. He stares at me. Nananannal!" She then went back to her not-so-ultra-sonic mode. "If he's weird then you're weirder and might I add, eerie. Remember that guy who used to come to my shop when you were helping me out? You found out that he liked you so you thought it would be fun to just stare at him bluntly till you creeped him out. He still looks behind him when he leaves my shop. Remember the time you had severe anemia and you looked like that little girl from The Ring with that white and black peasant dress you were wearing? Customers thought that you were my cousin Psycho Suzy from the asylum. Don't tell me that he's weird, you're just eerie and it's fun. You see, you stare at people to freak them out for fun but Castor stares at you because I think he likes you and you're his type."

"Yeah, Psycho Suzy was fun. Hahaha, remember that customer who decided to pay for his books cash instead of installments because you told him that I was going to be working there for a while?" I ignored her last statement.

"Yeah, that was fun! But back to Castor. I'm serious." *Shit.* Her face was deadpan.

"Look, you're right. But I'm not looking for any male companion. I'm still getting over Michael."

"But you don't like Michael *that way*. You like Castor *that way*. And to tell you the truth, I know he shot you and all. But I have a feeling that you were meant to meet him. My tarot cards don't lie."

"Here we go again with the tarot cards. I must give you credit, it's been six months since you've said anything about them or your shoes. Babe, listen, I'll think about it. I'm just tired and you have to go to work."

"Alright, take care. Mwah! Don't forget to take your cell phone to the shower with you." She gave me a peck on the cheek and left.

I dragged myself upstairs and the first thing I did was put my cell phone on the shampoo stand inside the shower. My father had made a point that I take it with me in the shower so that if I slip or aliens came and abducted me, I'd be able to call him. He even had me sit on the floor of the shower in order to insert the stand at arm's length. I wasn't using the bathtub these days because I just didn't want to be alone with my thoughts.

I undressed as quickly as possible and for the first time in months, I actually looked at myself in the mirror. I had a scar from the bullet and some patchwork from surgeries that were barely visible. I stepped into the shower and the hot water pressure was great. I enjoyed the sound of water crashing around me in the shower. I didn't realize how long my hair had gotten over the past couple of months. It was longer than Castor's now.

Stupid hot FBI agent who shoots eerie undertakers. I couldn't help but remember his scent – musky white roses. What guy smells like that? And that hair, who has red blondish hair like that? He was not a ginger per se. Strawberry blonde maybe? But it was more reddish...mmm... I didn't like blondes either. Hell, no. And what's with those eyes, where did he get them from? The queen's crown jewels? I mean did he just steal her emerald stones and just stuffed them into his corneas thus using them as irises? I didn't understand the fascination. Did I mention that I only like tall, dark and mysterious men? I also love dark brown eyes. The darker the better.

No, no Polly. Don't go down that road, it's one thing that your friend turned into a terrorist and it's another that you like a guy who shot you. Man, what's wrong with me? I'm a sick masochist. I need professional help. That's right, nothing wrong with professional help. I was going to talk myself into making a martini and just watch some trash TV.

I got out the shower, put on a fluffy robe and ran downstairs to make myself a martini. *One-part vermouth, three parts vodka and three olives.* I told myself. My father had entered the kitchen and just gawked at me.

"Drinking in the afternoon and wearing a robe, having problems, are we?"

"I'm going to take a nap after that. I assume Lieutenant York told you what happened?" I smiled.

"Yeah, I knew you would go home so I'm taking a long lunch break to eat with you. Do you mind pouring one finger of scotch while I grill the steaks?"

"No, problem. Dad can't you fix me a grilled cheese sandwich like all the other daddies?"

"No, because unlike all the daddies I prefer to feed my daughters meat. And if it weren't for the meat, you wouldn't be able to survive. Meat makes you strong." He winked at me. My father wrote the book on old wives' tales.

"I don't think the grilled cheese sandwich would've tasted good anyways with the martini." I smiled faintly. I did not like looking sad in front of my father.

"So, Vince and Lieutenant York tell me that you dropped the charges against Castor Black?"

"Umm, yeah. You think I shouldn't have done that?"

"Well, you remember Francis Prique the investigator?"

"Yes, I do. I thought he was working on my case, but I didn't see him today."

"Oh, he's still working on your case, but he had to undergo surgery, minor procedure- that's why Lieutenant York was there. Francis should be back to work tomorrow. Don't worry though, York is keeping him updated. Anyhow, Francis told me about Michael, his dad, his girlfriend, her dad and about Castor.

To be frank Sweetie, this is a big shit hole and you were very noble about letting Castor go. Francis was very touched by your gesture, so was Lieutenant York, Eddie, Vince and the agents there. Sandy Black even gave me a call thanking me. I told him that I had nothing to do with this, that it was all you. Your mom, rest in peace, would have done the exact same thing because she was one classy lady. Truth be told, I was just at Salt and Pepper Catering. These steaks were a gift from Sandy. The guy doesn't know what to do in order to thank you. Castor is on modified duty and is under probation. I am sure he would have lost his job if he were found guilty in front of a jury. I have no doubt he would be for reckless endangerment. They are keeping a lot of things under wraps."

"I know, Dad. I was kind of unexpected collateral damage. But if I had died or worse been paralyzed, you wouldn't be so understanding now, would you?" I couldn't help but feel a bit hurt. I kept a straight face.

"Don't ever think that I'm ok with the fact that you almost died, and I made it clear to everyone at the field office and my job. But shit happens sometimes and you're ok. What do you want me to do? I honestly blame Michael! This is his fault. He chose to do something bad while you were around! I raised that boy and he was like a son to me. He was *my son*. I lost a son. And I feel guilty for how he turned out. I keep asking myself what I could have done differently. I cannot place the whole blame on Castor or the FBI. They were doing their job. But, thank God you are ok. Castor stopped a bomb from going off!" My father was all huffy now. I went into the house and poured him that one finger of scotch. I came back out and handed it to him. He was keeping an eye on the steaks.

"I saw his brother at mom's funeral, how come Castor didn't recognize me on the bus? He met me in person that day."

"I asked him that and Castor told him that you looked very different to him the day he saw you on the bus. He said something about your hair covering your eyes almost and that you had very long hair. Your hair was in a bun at your mom's funeral. He was wearing sunglasses that day because he had an eye infection and didn't want to gross people out and you know the rest of the story. If he had told Sandy about the eye infection, he wouldn't have let him work that day. He only helped him deliver the food to the location. There were two helpers who set the buffet."

"Ugh, whatever. Never knew a makeover could almost get a girl killed."

My dad laid two pieces of steak on my plate. I had put together a tomato salad. I loved black tomatoes. We finished our late lunch and my dad left back to work. I went back upstairs with my martini and put it on a coaster on my nightstand. I threw on my Corpse Bride pajamas. It had been a long day.

I couldn't forget the look in Michael's eyes when I punched him. I couldn't forget his chilling words. Anne told me that they brought in Julia, Michael's mom, for questioning. The worrisome situation is all this; Julia has been MIA for almost three weeks. She hasn't been answering neither her cell nor house phone. She was not even home. No lights, no car in the driveway- No one has been around that house for almost three weeks. The police and FBI were working together. They have been watching our home and hers during this time. My father had already hired an assistant for Anne.

I woke up at 6 p.m. a little light-headed. I heard voices downstairs and assumed Anne and my father were home from work. I went downstairs and my sister was watching some soap opera. She barely noticed me. Dad was in the kitchen with his 'crayons' coloring and drawing.

"How are you doing, kiddo?"

"Good, light-headed though."

"I just made a pot of fresh coffee for Anne. But it seems she's thinking or something. She has a lot on her hands. Julia's disappearance is very peculiar."

I went to the counter and poured myself some coffee. I saw an envelope with no postal stamp and no sender address. I turned to my Dad and asked him if he knew anything about it.

"Dad what's this?" Holding up the envelope.

"Oh, yeah, I almost forgot. Castor passed by me at work today and asked me if I could give you this envelope. I didn't open it and Vince said it was ok. So, open it."

Feeling perplexed, I opened the envelope and in there was a check for $25,000 with a letter. I showed it to my father, and he wasn't surprised. I didn't bother opening the letter.

"Dad? You knew about this?" Placing the check on his drawing as an interruption.

"Actually, no, but I saw it coming. Castor feels very bad. I think he just gave you all his liquid assets. I think you should take it. It's the least he could do. You've been out of work and you're too much of a stubborn bull to take money from me. Uncle James and I are taking care of medical bills with the FBI but still you deserve some sort of monetary compensation. They paid for almost everything in the end, so we returned most of Uncle James' money. I mean, I don't totally forgive Castor but he's trying."

The money would come in handy for me. I had other expenses from moving back home and being out of work for so long. Still, I was not going to take it. I just can't. I would find a way. Anne and I had to give up our apartment and move back home to help Dad take care of Mom. Years ago, we had moved out when Anne turned 17. She wanted to study fashion and the institute was so far away from home. The only way my father would let her live alone if only I lived with her. Dad had a 'no dorms' policy. We never gave up the apartment after she finished studying because it was rent controlled. Anyways, we spent half the time home with Mom and Dad. It was the perfect balance of having a private and family life. I was barely at the rental anyways because of my corporate job. That was another life.

"Oh, come on Dad. I don't need this. If he thinks that if he gives me his money, that'll make him feel better about himself. I don't think so. I'm taking this money and giving it back to him."

"Whatever you decide I'm okay with it."

I took the letter and the check upstairs with me. I didn't want to open the letter. I didn't think he'd have anything important to say. *Ok, I might have lied.* So, I just opened the folded A4 paper.

Dear Polly,

I'm sorry if I've hurt your feelings in any way. You didn't give me a chance to say anything to you that's why I'm writing this letter. Words escaped me the last time I saw you to no fault of your own. I know the money is not that much – Just please take it. No need to complicate things. There isn't a day that goes by where I don't feel guilty. I keep replaying the events in my head. Internal Affairs are having a field day with me. They understand that it was a delicate situation, but they have a job to do as well.

I really didn't recognize you on the bus. I never forget a face. You looked like a different person. I never expected to see a girl who would try to take on an assailant like that. You are probably the bravest and toughest girl I've ever met, not to forget crazy because you didn't even think about yourself.

I know this money should be able to help you in a small way. I'm really thankful that you're getting better and if you ever need anything, you know where to find me. Finally, thank you for forgiving me and last, I won't let anyone hurt you. I made that promise to your dad. He said he'd like me more if I hadn't tried to kill his daughter by accident.

Your hole in the chest,

Castor

Nothing annoyed me about the letter but the part about being 'my hole in the chest'. *More like a hole in my head.* The biggest hole in my chest was Michael. Michael and Castor were my hole in my chest. Michael was a different kind of hole; he was the worst hole. The one where he just ripped my heart out and smeared it on his ballet slippers to give them a red tone. Was I not a good friend to him? Was I not a good listener? Did I do something wrong to screw him so bad? Maybe this was my fault. I passed my fingers along Castor's handwriting 'Your hole in the chest', he actually knew what I was talking about, not about my physical hole but my metaphoric hole. Stupid asshole. *Both.*

Three weeks had passed and still no Michael. The FBI had taken over his house and his mother was still missing. I saw Castor at Serenity's bookshop twice, but he didn't see me because I'd run to the back room when he came in. He told her that he had a hearing. Vince told me that he had been cleared and that my testimony at a private hearing did him good. Serenity didn't let me give him back the money, so I just put it in a savings account. I was scheduled to go back to work. I needed to go back to work. I missed Marc and Angelo, Uncle James, the quiet coroner and the rest of the staff. I mostly missed working with the dead. It had been my last physical therapy session that day and for some reason, Serenity wouldn't shut up about me giving Castor a call.

"Seriously, Polly, why don't you give him a call?"

"Seriously, why should I? and if you tell me that it was an unfortunate/fateful juxtaposition that brought us together, I think I'm going rip my own head off."

"How is it possible that you can rip your own head off?"

"Well, maybe I'd just be able to snap my hyoid and bruise my bones, whatever, I'll make a noose out of my hair and hang myself...you get the picture."

"That's still not ripping your head off. That's hanging yourself. Are we still on tonight? It's my birthday and all." She winked.

"Yeah of course, my car's been fixed, and I'll see you at club Thingy at nine."

"You're not driving there. Somebody is going to pick you up."

"Who? And why wouldn't I drive myself?"

"Well, you just had two hours of intense physical therapy and I want you to be in your full strength. My shop employee is picking you up."

"Alright whatever. I'll see you later." I gave her a peck on the cheek and went into the house. All the lights were on. Seemed like Dad wasn't big on saving the planet that day. I was sure Anne was home too. She probably came home to have dinner and go. She was invited to a fashion show tonight with her assistant. *Ladeedee ladeeda.* I entered the living room and dad was preparing some finger food, he is having the guys over tonight for poker I assumed. I went upstairs to take a shower. It took me forever to pick out what I was going to wear. It had been a long time since I went out partying. I decided to wear a slashed cotton black blouse with spider web lace. A black skirt and a studded belt. I wore my knee-high midnight blue Doctor Martens. I wore my black corset coat. I didn't feel like wearing any lipstick tonight, so I just played around with my midnight blue eye shadow and black liquid eyeliner. I just brushed my hair. I usually do nothing with it. I was in dire need of a haircut though. It was long as my skirt. I took a pair of scissors and went downstairs to my dad.

"Daddy, please?" I started making snipping sounds for him.

"No way, over my dead body."

"I can arrange that you know. But if you're dead you wouldn't be able to use scissors. Besides, you shave your head, so you don't know what it feels like. I mean if you're growing my hair to then cut it and use it as plugs then I don't mind."

"Young lady, I don't care how pissed you're trying to make me. I'm not cutting it. And I shave my head because it's too perfect to cover." He stuck his tongue at me.

I grunted and stomped upstairs. *Yes, like a teenager. No, I couldn't cut my own hair. I'll probably tell you why someday. Yes, it's embarrassing.*

Dad was being mean. Why couldn't he forbid me from doing other things like normal daddies do, like not playing with dead animals and turning our backyard into an animal cemetery. My father could never bear to see a scissor snip through my hair. It was like making him sit and listen to a vegan's theories on why he shouldn't eat things with a face and that fish had feelings.

It was 8:15 p.m. and I was expecting Serenity's employee to pick me up any minute. I was in the kitchen having a cup of coffee with my dad while we made it clear that he was rubber and I was glue. There was a knock on the door. My dad got up to answer the it. The guy was so tall that he blocked the entrance. I still couldn't see Serenity's assistant.

"Hey, didn't expect to see you here. Is everything ok?"

"I'm sorry, Mr. Deuce. I'm invited to Serenity's party and she asked me, well, demanded that I pick up Polly."

12

I recognized that voice. My father moved so that I could see who it was. I expected someone else but not him.

It was Castor Black. Dad moved to the side of the doorframe welcoming him in. Dad patted him on the back. He came to my table, placing a pack of Twinkies wrapped with a red bow and said: "Serenity told me that they're your favorite sugary snack."

I didn't know whether to smile because I love Twinkies or because he took the time to wrap a bow around them. Moreover, what is he doing here? The simple perplexities of situations are a pain in my neck. *Don't worry. I didn't smile.* Complicated me, gave nothing away. *Resting bitch face it is.*

"Ummm...thank you. But you're not supposed to pick me up, her employee was supposed to pick me up. What are you doing here?" I frowned.

"That is true but George got a flat tire, so she called me to pick you up." *He'd better wipe that grin off his face. Smug bastard.*

I smiled sarcastically. "Yeah, and she couldn't find anybody but *you* to pick me up."

"Well, she didn't want to leave you stranded and wind up taking a cab with all that's going on. Now, you have no choice because she told me that she would kick my FBI ass to the curb and would refuse service to me if I ever came to her shop. You see, there's a lot to consider and to be honest, she scares me a bit."

I mumbled. "I'm the one who's going to kick her ass to the curb."

"Okay, are you ready to go?" I hated it when people interrupted my mumbling.

"Yeah, but my dad won't let me go with you. You know shooting his daughter and all." I turned to my dad for support. My dad reciprocated with the following: "I have no problem Polly, let bygones be bygones. I'm not one to hold a grudge and Castor has been very decent in all this. Besides, he's an agent and he can protect you if anything were to happen, like Michael appearing for instance. And Sweetie, try not to imagine yourself smacking me on the head with a Teflon pan because I can see it in your eyes, and I love you." He smiled at me.

Catholics and their forgiveness…overrated.

I grunted and gave in. "Okay dad, but know this, if I die tonight, I'm going to haunt you and you'll never be able to eat any meat again."

Both, my dad and Castor laughed, then my dad said: "The haunting I understand, the meat-eating part is what I don't get, I don't think there's anything you can do to make meat repulsive to me."

"I'll make sure your meat will always be well-done. I will haunt your grill."

"That is repulsive." He started mumbling about people eating well-done meat should might as well throw it in the garbage. I really needed to get going even if it was with Castor. I didn't want to be late for Serenity's funeral…I mean birthday.

Gonna kill her.

"Dad, I'm going to have to leave now. Have fun. Say hi to the guys for me. I love you, *you* crazy man." I stood on my toes to give him a peck on the cheek.

"Love you too, my twisted disgusting child." He gave me a bear hug.

Castor and I walked to his car. He had a 2008 BMW 3 series. It was a sleek black color. I never had him for a German car lover. My dad was still standing at the door and shouted to us. "Have a good time kids and Castor, if you return Polly back home in less than the perfect shape that she is, I will use your intestines for sausages. You'd be awake for the process as well." My dad winked at him. *As for me, disgusted. Can this situation be any more embarrassing?*

We got in the car and we both buckled up. He put the car in reverse in the driveway and we left. His car smelled like him, white musky rose. It had a matte black interior. A complete contrast to the shiny sleek exterior. He probably had a polish fetish like Michael. *Michael... No, Polly. We are not thinking about him tonight.* A few minutes later, he asked: "So, what's your music style?"

"Well, I prefer metal. I love European metal bands."

He turned his head to me. "Seriously? I'm a big fan. Ever heard of Macbeth?"

Stop being so perfect.

"Yes, my favorite album is Romantic Tragedy's Crescendo."

"Oh yeah, there's this song on it called The Dark Kiss of My Angel."

"Yeah, I actually love Thy Mournful Lover. I love the whole album. It speaks to me. The lyrics are just simple and straight to the point."

"It's very goth. Umm...Would you like me to crank up the heat a bit?"

What just happened?

"No, I'm fine. It's actually a tad bit too hot."

Why the hell does he think I'm cold? I looked down at my arms. Why the hell am I crossing my arms? I'm all types of weird right now.

"Oh, my bad. So, it seems we have one thing in common." He was so focused on the road and barely looking at me.

"Listen, I don't mean to be a bitch, but we have nothing in common. You're just taking me to the party because Serenity sprung this upon you. I'll have someone take me back. Nothing more. I am sorry she put you in this situation and had I known, I would have taken a cab." I was so uncomfortable. I could feel my

ears turning red.
There I go being rude and weird.

"Hey, take it easy. What I meant by common is our musical taste. I rarely know anyone who likes European metal. I just mentioned Macbeth from the top of my head. Didn't expect you to know them. I do not want you to feel any unease, alright? But whether you like it or not, I am taking you back for your own safety and we don't have to talk if that's what you want. I see that I somewhat irritate you. You are afraid. It is understandable due to the circumstances."
Bastard shut me up without having to argue with me. What is wrong with this man? *Get out of my head! My heart was going boom..boom…boo…boo..boomm…boodoom…booom….bbbb-bbbooooooommmmm!*
He drew a long unfulfilled breath. "You could never be a bitch, Polly."
Beeeeeeeeeeeeeeeeeeeep! I flat-lined right then and there.

I couldn't say anything to that. I was just anxious to get out of the car.
As we got out of the car, I remembered something. "Did George give you Serenity's present? I had him pick it up for her from this novelty shop."

He opened his car trunk and handed it to me. "He told me to pass by him to get it. I left my present inside with the others."
Huh? How? What? Nevermind.

Again, I said nothing. I then noticed something. He was wearing pleather pants, not those tacky ones. He was wearing a white shirt and a black pleather tie. He had a black scarf draped around his neck. His belt buckle was interesting though, it had a triquetra engraved on it. His hair was shorter, down to his shoulder blades. It was the first time I saw his hair fall freely. He usually tied it. The contrast of his leather trench coat made his hair look ash blonde with a hint of red. His eye rims were lined with kohl. It looked great with his green eyes. *Fuck my life.*

As we walked in, he put his hand lightly on the small of

my back to make our way through the crowd. I turned around to face him. "Could you please keep your hands to yourself?" Oh my God, he's going to think I am one of those women who think they are all that.

He half-smiled. "Polly, I'm just leading you through the crowd. I'm sorry it's involuntary. Comes with the territory." He put his hand down immediately. We spotted Serenity's table and she looked gorgeous. She had her red hair in a retro style do. There were a lot of people at her table. She had reserved three tables. Everyone loved Serenity. She stood up to greet me and I gave her a hug. "You're so lucky that there are witnesses so I can't brutally murder you." I whispered in her ear. "You're welcome and I love you too. Did you check out his butt in those pants? Wait till he takes off his coat." She whispered back in my ear and started laughing. She sat me down next to Castor *naturally*. She was pushing her luck too far.

What was she expecting? I know that she meant well but I just was in a weird way, afraid of him, afraid of falling in love with him. All this didn't make sense to me. I could still hear his voice in my head when I got shot. The way he hugged me was so loving and caring. I felt peace. I handed Serenity her present and she was so happy with it. I had bought her a vintage crystal perfume bottle, with a pump and everything. She had a thing for perfume and vintage perfume bottles. I had seen it two months prior to my accident and knew that I had to buy it for her. She gave me a peck on the cheek. I was happy that she loved it. Castor gifted her a Pashmina.

It was crowded that evening. The rock band was good. They played some real oldies. I couldn't recognize a lot of them. The food was great. Everyone at the party enjoyed themselves and I was enjoying myself as well. George, Serenity's shop assistant, arrived a bit late but everyone was glad to see him. Serenity's cake was to die for, it was a chocolate frosted velvet cake topped with red roses. It was a decent cake, honestly. I mention this- for the cake at her last year's bash was a macabre of melted buttercream. She cried in the bathroom and I was almost arrested for threatening the bakery. No one messes with my friend, especially on her birthday.

"Serenity, this cake is so good. You have to give me the name of your bakery."

"Sweetie, it's not a bakery."

"Bakery, patisserie, or whatever."

She looked at me then at Castor. "I do make one hell of a chocolate frosted velvet cake, don't I?" He said aloud in front of everybody. *I can't catch a fuckin break, can I?* "Yeah, it's good." I then excused myself from the table to get a refill. There was no way I was going to get through this night without some fluid valor.

The band was playing soft rock songs, and everyone was slow dancing. There was a couple at the adjacent table exchanging amylase and another at our table who had too much to drink- the girlfriend threw up on her boyfriend. That was funny. I grinned, I couldn't help it.

"Not everyone can hold their liquor." Castor smiled.

"Yeah, but the barfing on her boyfriend was funny." I laughed.

"True. I can't stand some men who wear pink. It is one of my pet peeves. I am not proud of myself."

"Me too. That's usually a nine on my barf-o-meter."

"Haha! You have a barf-o-meter. You're funny, Polly. But, you see, my dear, what she did to him surpasses any given number on any meter. I would call that a favor for all mankind."

"You're right. Now, you're the one who's funny." I smiled.

George had come up to apologize for not picking me up. He then asked me to dance with him and I did. He was a sweet guy and a very hard worker. Serenity treated him as if he were a friend and not just an employee. I obliged. It had been a long time since I'd danced.

"So, how are you doing, Polly? I hope you weren't annoyed with the fact that you came here with Castor." He asked.

"Well, yes. I just feel uncomfortable with him." He twirled me.

"I think he likes you. He was very excited to come pick you up. He didn't mind Serenity threatening him at all, if you know what I mean."

"Why does everyone keep telling me crap like this? George, Honey, the guy is an FBI agent; he shot me by accident. I'm just trying to be civil. Nothing's going to happen between me and him. He's not my type. Why is Serenity doing this to me?" I don't know how many octaves my voice went up. I swear to Lucifer I think this has become a conspiracy. It is not funny anymore. *Strike that.* It was never funny to begin with.

"Sweetie, she loves you and wants you to be happy, that's all. You know, she looks at things differently. Putting aside circumstances, he's a good person, Polly. I used to think he was weird with his eyeliner and black nail polish. I never expected him to be in law enforcement. He even cooks and helps his brother with the business. Look, if you're that annoyed, I'll talk to Serenity. Don't be mad at her, she loves you very much. You're just feeling overwhelmed and I can understand that."

Feeling overwhelmed...been hearing and feeling a lot of that lately.

"Thank you." I said and he kissed my hand. George was still the Southerner I had met a year ago. He was always polite with the ladies. Castor came out of nowhere and cut between us. "Do you mind?" He asked George. George stepped back and Castor held my hand and put his other hand on the small of my back. We swayed for a couple of seconds and then I stopped. We looked into each other's eyes. I exhaled and excused myself. I got my bag and went to the bathroom. I entered a stall and closed the lid of the seat and sat on it. My eyes watered. I got my emergency cigarette from the seam of my bag. I had given up cigarettes, but it was times like this that I needed one. I heard someone come in and I could tell from the footsteps that it was Serenity. I could hear her stop in front of my stall.

"Polly, I'm sorry. George told me while you were dancing with Castor how annoyed you were with me. Can you forgive me? There are no witnesses here if that helps." She said sheepishly.

"I thought I was angry with you but I'm not. I don't know what's wrong with me." I felt ashamed.

"Polly, I see how you look at each other. I'm sorry if I've overstepped my boundaries." I could hear from her voice that she was truly apologetic. She gasped. "Are you smoking?"

"Yes, I am. I'm not opening the door till I'm finished."

Yeah, it's illegal to smoke indoors. Sue me.

"Then you must be really crushing hard on this guy. I hope the smoke alarm doesn't go off."

"What? Baby, you had too much to drink. You know sugar and alcohol; not a good combination."

"I'm very sober, Miss Deuce. For you to feel the need to go and light a cigarette means that you are nervous. Castor makes you nervous." Again, with that smile in her voice. Thank goodness for the stall door. I wanted to strangle her, with love. She still was my friend.

I didn't answer her. She continued, "You know I'm right, that's why you're not answering." I then answered courtly, "I actually wanted to have my cigarette in peace." I opened the stall door. She stretched out her arms and gave me a hug. We washed our hands with half a bottle of antiseptic soap Serenity had in her bag. We went back out to the party. Castor came up and took me aside. *Not this again. Why does he have to smell so good?*

"Polly, are you alright?"

"Yes."

"What happened? Did I offend you in any way?"

"No."

"So, what's the matter?"

"Look, nothing's the matter and stop interrogating me." *Fuck my life. Again.*

"Fine, I'm sorry. I'll leave you alone now. When you're ready to go home, tell me."

He turned and sat down next to this girl from the party whom I didn't know. She was pretty but dressed like a librarian. Another martini later and several dances with George, Serenity, guy with blue hair, hot gay couple and then George again, I decided that I needed to call it a night. I probably had a bit too much to drink. Yes, I had had 5 martinis, *okay, 4 and a half martinis to be honest.* I wasn't drunk but I was getting the alcohol sweats and needed fresh air. I took my bag and went outside. There were a lot of people waiting outside. I asked the bouncer for a cigarette and he gave me one. I lit it and got my cell phone out in order to call a cab. A woman answered and as I was giving her directions someone grabbed my hand, instantly, I smacked him in the head with my bag that was in my left hand. *Oh, man. It was Castor.* Did he tag me with a locator or something?

"Didn't I tell you to tell me when you wanted to go home?"

"Yes." I rolled my eyes like a sixteen-year-old. I lit another cigarette for dramatic effect.

"So? What's this *and ouch*, what the hell do you carry in that bag?" He was rubbing his head.

"I decided not to tell you. Listen, you're not my father or my boyfriend. You can't tell me what to do." *No one could tell me what to do, ask my dad.*

"I want to keep you safe. We still haven't found Michael."

"He'd never hurt me intentionally."

"He already did." He just stared at me. "Now, let me take you home. You look wiped and, might I add, tipsy."

I put out my cigarette and followed him to the car. We got in and left. I started feeling very queasy and wished he would stop the car. *Okay, I was going to hurl.* I put my hand on his while he was changing gears. He immediately understood. He brought the car to a halt and parked it on the side of the road. I got out and tried to walk as fast as possible because he needn't see my stomach contents, I had that reserved for movie night. I puked my guts out and felt better. I told him to stay away between projectiles. I felt so much better. I walked, wobblingly, back to the car and he wasn't in his seat. I squatted placing my hand on the car as to not lose balance. I heard his trunk close and he came to my side. He kneeled next to me and gave me a bottle of water.

"Here's some water."

"Thank you." He stood up again and walked to his seat. I rinsed my mouth and spat on the ground then took a small sip of water. I stood up slowly and got in the car. I closed the door and opened my bag, luckily, there was a stick of gum. I unwrapped it and popped the damn thing in my mouth. Thank God it was mint. I focused on chewing. I could only hear the thrumming of the engine in my stupor. He drove slowly and there was some traffic. I saw that there was a checkpoint set up by the police. I didn't bother to ask. He put his hand on my hand to get my attention.

"Polly, there's a checkpoint here, nothing to worry about. They must be checking out license plates." He paused. "Are you alright? You look paler than usual."

"I'm fine. Just sleepy." I managed to say. I was so dizzy.

"Alright, close your eyes and rest. I need to park the car for a second on the side to see what's going on. There might be something going down."

"K." That was all I could manage. All the police cherries looked like Christmas lights. I tried not to fall asleep, but my lids were not responding.

I woke up to find myself in my bed. I was parched. I looked at my nightstand clock and it was two in the morning. Did I fall asleep in his car? How did I get upstairs? I looked under the covers and saw that I was wearing my pajamas. I rolled over and noticed that my TV was on. I raised my head and saw someone on my chaise longue. I turned on my night stand lamp and it was Castor. Our eyes met and he smiled. *Oh, Hell no!*

"How are you feeling Miss Deuce?" He was either mocking me or being sincere. I could not tell.

"I'm alright. What the hell are you doing here in my room, in my house, at this hour? Did you undress me!?" I hissed between my teeth.

I was a hair breadth away from reaching a certain level of homicidal lividness.

"No, Anne deprived me of that joy. We came here at 1 a.m. You were in deep sleep and I didn't want to wake you. Your father was asleep, so I carried you upstairs and Anne dressed you. I stood outside. But I did pick out your sleepwear. You have a very fascinating wardrobe. Besides, you looked sickly and your sister let me stick around just to make sure you're ok. She even made me a cup of black coffee. Bless her heart." He reminisced as if this happened six months ago. I wanted to remodify his face.

"Ok, thank you. Can you please go?" I whispered.

"Well, I haven't finished my coffee." He was sipping his coffee stridently.

"Take it with you." I bit my upper lip as to not get colorful with my language.

"I don't have a coffee cup holder in my car."

"You're a cop and don't have a coffee cup holder in your car?" I almost chuckled.

"First, I'm an FBI agent. Second, I don't drink coffee in my car. I like to avoid spills and I hate travel mugs."

"Then what the hell are you drinking your coffee from?"

"Your sister poured my coffee in this paper cup. She wanted to keep the kitchen sink immaculate. Poor thing was tired, so I made an exception. Didn't want to be an asshole. Speaking of cups, you had way too much to drink."

Martinis don't come in cups.

"I had like five martinis. I didn't even finish the last one."

"Well, you had too many tequila shots. That's what threw off your balance. I was just worried about you."

"I'm ok now, please go home or I'm going to clobber you."

"You can't clobber an agent. People go to jail for that."

"Not if I charge him with trespassing private property."

"Your sister let me in, and you were passed out."

"Good God, please leave. I want to sleep."

"Alright, go to sleep. Make believe I'm not here. I'm almost done with my coffee. Oh, and here's a glass of water. Pretty sure you need it." He exulted.

He handed me the glass of water. He sat back on the chaise longue. I realized he was watching the news on mute. He then switched off the TV. My nightstand lamp was still on. He sat straight and just stared at me. I hated it when he stared at me. His eyes looked too intense.

"What now?" I asked.

"Nothing. Go back to sleep. Would you like me to get you anything before I leave?"

"No. Thank you."

He got up and turned off the lamp. I rolled over and buried my head in my pillow. A few minutes later, I got up to use the bathroom. I came back in and noticed that he had forgotten his scarf on the chaise. I took it with me to bed and smelled it into oblivion. *I know, I do sick weird things sometimes.*

13

It was Monday and my first day back at work. I spent Sunday with Serenity and some Aspirin. I told her about my night, in my bedroom with Castor. She wasn't happy about the fact that there was no action. I made it a point numerous times that this was all her fault. She dismissed me over red velvet cheesecake, Cuban coffee and reruns of Mexican soap operas. We understood squat without subtitles, but that Soraya Montenegro character was a devious melodramatic diva. She knew how to have a proper meltdown. I needed one of those. She was officially my spirit animal.

My dad had invited all his friends from work to a barbecue. Everyone was there, Francis Prique, Lieutenant York, Vince and his Ball. I couldn't remember who else. Serenity and I spent most of the day in my bedroom. Anne used me as a dummy for her latest project. But someone forgot to mention to her that I wasn't a pin cushion. The kid still can't pin fabric properly on a human being. I gave her hell about Castor and the coffee; I then forgave her after she chased me around the house trying fit me in a pink dress.

I was so excited to go back to work. It felt like my first day back at school when I was a kid, minus the smell of the new plastic covers for books and pencil cases. My mother would take us mid-August to purchase our strawberry-scented erasers from the school supplies shop. We started saving for school supplies once we were out for the summer. It made my sister and I appreciate our skull pencil cases more. I put on my steel toed Doctor Martens, threw on a pair of low-cut waist jeans and a black turtle neck. I wore my long pleather trench coat and French braided my very long hair.

Anne and my father had already left for work early that morning. I grabbed a cup of coffee and spread some cream cheese on a slice of rye bread. I left the house and got into my car. I hadn't used my car since my accident. My dad redid the upholstery while I was in a coma. He hasn't forgiven himself for not picking me up from work that day. I put on the heater and backed my car out of the driveway. It started to rain as I reached an intersection. There was a homeless guy putting up his card-board box home. When I got to work, Uncle James was at the reception greeting me.

"Welcome back, kiddo. We've missed you here. How are you feeling? Any stiffness?" He hugged me hesitantly. Everyone had been doing that lately except for my father. The only person who was still treating me normal.

"I'm fine, Uncle James. Thanks. I'm going to punch in and go see Marc."

"Alright then, I'll give you the roster later."

"Okay."

I walked quickly to the embalming room. I had missed that place. I opened the door and there was the whole staff with balloons and ribbons. I saw a Welcome Back banner. There were drinks and cake. I couldn't believe it. Uncle James came right behind me and gave me a hug. *That hug was a bit tighter. Much better*. Angelo handed me a tombstone locket engraved with the words: "Not today." He hugged me and lifted me off the floor. Marc came into the room and gave me a present as well. It was his version of Raggedy Anne, she was stiff and embalmed. "I made her a coffin." Uncle James said. We all laughed. Our coroner was there too. She had baked the cake herself. I realized that Uncle James had recruited more people. *I was still the only female undertaker. I felt a little let down. I didn't know why.*

"Marc, the funeral is tomorrow morning. It's 5:30, why

haven't you finished yet?"

"The son of a bitch's skin is really ugly. I've tried two types of creams and still those damn craters show up on his face."

"Can't you get him a death mask or something?" I said jokingly. He was about to have an aneurysm from all the stress he was under.

"I wish but then I wouldn't have a job. So, how was your first day back? Were you able to dig without trouble? Angelo told me that you looked as if nothing happened to you. Knock on wood."

"That's true but I still feel weak in some places. My chest muscles are still a bit tight, not painful though. You would think using a front hoe excavator would make the job easier. But no, you still have to dig a lot of corners manually."

"I hear you. Angelo refuses to use that excavator sometimes, especially around those big statues. On the other hand, didn't physical therapy work out for you?" He was still dabbling with some makeup for Crater Face.

"Oh yes, it did. I don't think I would've been able to come back to this line of work if it didn't."

"Well, why don't you try Yoga? It's good for your body and mind. Angelo was having some mild discomfort in his back. Nothing worked I tell you. He started attending this Yoga class with me and he's never complained since."

"You and Angelo do Yoga?" I giggled like a school girl. One should understand; Angelo comes from a long line of Italians and they love their pasta, heavy workout gym machines and wine. Paleo-diets, workout fads and stretching is the equivalent of him seeing someone put ketchup on a slice of pizza.

"Yes, come on it'll be fun. I started Yoga because as you can see you, me and everyone else's livelihood here, depends on touching and looking at the dead. I need to see some people are not going into rigor mortis."

"I see. I don't have physical therapy anymore, but I'll have to think about it." I looked down at the cadaver he was working on. "Marc, you made him look like Mickey Rourke post botched plastic surgery."

"Yeah, so what? Mickey Rourke is happening even with the botched face lift." We both laughed. We both loved Mickey Rourke.

I went back outside to finish digging another plot for another funeral we were holding tomorrow at 4 p.m. I felt a tightness in my chest and stopped. I sat down and removed my gloves. Angelo and the new guy came up to me.

"Polly, are you ok?" Angelo asking warily.

"Yeah, it's just my chest. It feels a bit tight."

"Take deep breaths. You dug three plots today, all by yourself. That's too much for your first day back at work. Let one of those newbies do the job, you just supervise."

"Angelo, it's my job. I'm fine now."

"Mr. Roberts hired more people for the work load. He's purchased three lots to be used as a private cemetery. So, don't worry about anything. The newbies need your expertise."

"Alright, it's time for me to go anyways." I looked at the new guy and said: "Who are you?"

He had very curious eyes.

"I'm Elijah. I'm an undertaker too. Is there anything you'd like me to do Miss Deuce?"

"Please call me Polly. Did you purchase a few yards of carpet grass for tomorrow?"

"No, I didn't. Is that part of my job description as well?"

"Yes, Elijah. It is. You should fill out a purchase order and give it to Mrs. Sophia in Purchasing. Anything you need to buy she needs to approve it for you. Got that?"

"Yes. I'll go in now and make sure they'll have them delivered first thing tomorrow morning. But we used to just plant the grass at my old job. It took like one to two weeks depending on the weather."

"I understand but we don't do that here. Mr. Roberts doesn't like to see dirt on his plots. My shift's over. It was nice meeting you."

Angelo cleared his throat and turned to Elijah. "Miss Deuce is an excellent undertaker. She's been here a long time. Do as she says, besides' he paused ', you answer to her or me."

"Alright, Angelo. Let me finish up." Elijah excused himself and left.

"What do you mean answer to *her* or me? You're my supervisor." I asked confusingly.

"Well, Polly. You set up the accounting system when you first got here in exchange for learning this vocation. Mr. Roberts isn't going to find a better qualified undertaker than you. I told him that I needed you as my assistant supervisor because I wasn't going to let him stick me with one of those newbies who can't keep their lunch down if things get messy. We haven't even scheduled orientation. Please understand my stance."

"Angelo, I'm just happy with being an undertaker. I can't take on more responsibility right now, you know, with all that's happened with me."

"Polly, you deserve this. I've known you ever since I started working here. Mr. Roberts bought three more pieces of land and he wants you and I to give him ideas about where we should build mausoleums, crypts and angel statues. Come on, you love those things."

"Yeah, you know I do." I tugged him. "But why didn't Uncle James tell me this? And shouldn't he be hiring a landscaper or some architectural firm for this?"

"An architectural landscaping firm is going to be working with us. We need to give them a vision. Mr. Roberts has a lot on his plate. So here we are. He didn't want you to feel pressured by him. I told him not to tell you anything." He scratched his chin.

"Alright, I accept if I get to have a say in the mausoleums and angels." I said jokingly.

"And extra pay." He winked at me.

I punched out and walked straight to my car. It started raining again. I couldn't help but get flashbacks of the last day I saw Michael. He had been waiting outside to take me home.

Some minutes later, he was trying to blow up the city. I also remembered his last words to me on that day when he was just Michael: *"But, know one thing that you mean a lot to me and I would never do anything to jeopardize our friendship."* My brain refused to affiliate him with the Michael I saw that day in the clinic's bathroom stall. It was the first time I had ever hit him with the intention of inflicting pain. I felt the same tightness in my chest again with that God-awful lump in my throat. *No, I will not cry.*

I got in my car and started the engine. I checked my visor mirror. I imagined seeing him in the back seat. I couldn't shake the words he told me that day in the clinic's bathroom.

"I can't be a performer forever. There's a shelf life to what I do. I don't want to live a mediocre life and have a mediocre family with mediocre friends. Clarabel's dad has taken me in as if I were his son. They fight for a cause and have many beliefs and as you know I am Russian and Clarabel is half Russian. As you know, Russians live mediocre lives here unless they are part of a group. They go to Russia and learn ballet and come back here and take our jobs. Ballet dancing is by nature mostly than by nurture. I have failed Clarabel's father with this operation and yes, it was a bomb and it was meant to go off. It was just to send a message to a few people. How the hell was I supposed to know that a rogue agent was working undercover with them for three years? I had just met him two months before the incident"

The whole thing still echoed in my head. I didn't like the way he used the word 'mediocre'. I wondered if he ever considered our friendship to be mediocre. There was nothing, to my knowledge, mediocre or average about our friendship to that fact. I turned on my car's CD player and there it was; a CD Michael had bought for me before my mother died. It was a compilation of Gustav Mahler's greatest works. We needed a break from the Russian composers. I ejected the CD and opened my car window. I broke the CD in half and threw it out the window. I closed the window and backed up my car. Tears welled up in my eyes. *No, I will not cry.*

I was on my way to Serenity's shop. I was in dire need of

a good book. I stopped at a red light and reached for my glove compartment. I got out the first CD that I was able to grab and inserted it in the player. It was a mix doom metal CD. I had forgotten what was on that thing. The first song that came on was The Dark Kiss of My Angel by Macbeth. *Oh, come on!* Why is my CD player hating on me today? Why can't it magically burn music that may cause me heartbreak? I opted to listen to the song. Castor didn't seem like the guy who would like that song. I was listening attentively to the lyrics. The light turned green. I remembered how once Michael didn't appreciate the female vocals and the male's growling. What did he know? Their unique voices complemented the lyrics. I no longer wished to torture myself and lowered the volume.

For some reason, that song reminded me of the day that I got shot. It was the first time that I was able to literally relate to that song. The vocalists had heavy accents which made it even more mystical.

Stupido ballerino. I sighed.

I arrived at Serenity's shop and it was still pouring. I ran from my car to her shop. Man, there were a lot of customers today. I think she had just received her pile of erotic books. She mostly sold vintage books but brought many 'delicacies' from time to time and her prices were much better than those corporate giants. There were three stands for best-sellers. I'm telling you it was like people waiting in line for Cronuts. I walked straight to the back room and there was Serenity with her head in her hands. She looked as if she were on the verge of a breakdown. *Wow, it was weird having roles switched.*

"Serenity, what's wrong? George and the cashier are being smothered by the clients outside!" I didn't see any other employee out there but him and the part time cashier.

"Polly! Thank God you're here! You have to help me please!"

"What? Tell me. Something the matter?"

"Yeah, the accounting. Something's wrong with the system. My journal entries refuse to cooperate with my ledgers because my expense accounts decided to sleep with my revenues."

"Hahaha!" I laughed and she giggled. "Okay, go out front and I'll take care of this here. There probably was a glitch in system. I just hope that your journal entries wore protection."

"Very funny. Okay, I'm going out front. I put aside a few books that I think you might like. Be right back."

She left the room and I rearranged her invoices. After half an hour, it came to my attention that her system was automatically producing expense accounts and the revenues showed a negative number naturally. I traced it back to the journal entries, but I couldn't find what was wrong. It dawned upon me that her system wasn't automatically producing the numbers in the ledgers. I reset the system, and everything was working smoothly. But still the expense accounts wouldn't give in. So, I just erased the double entries and made up a sample entry and entered it. It didn't give double entries. I restarted the computer and it worked. The whole ordeal took almost an hour. Thank God she didn't need the software company to come and fix it. Those bastards usually charged an arm and a leg to the company I used to work with.

I went up front to give Serenity the good news and she was ecstatic. I told her that she should train George and the cashier properly with the program because there were some mistakes in the entries. I think it was a bug. They shouldn't use the accounting computer for the internet anymore.

The crowd of customers was dwindling. I was beginning to see more and more of the shop again. When Serenity purchased this shop after a lawsuit she won, it was an antique shop. She had decided to keep the décor because it fitted with her business concept. I remember the day when we bought that old cash register from the flea market. It still worked, and she used it. George was rearranging the books and the last client had purchased five erotic books.

"Well, as they say, sex sells."

"You think? These books are rare. They don't bring them at those corporate chains. I don't know why. I read them and they are erotic, I mean it's not even porn. It's erotic romance. Vintage books."

"Of course, they aren't going to sell something like that. They have much more important books like pop stars' bios and political conspiracy crap."

"Yeah, you're right. It's as if no one knows how to just get laid anymore."

"Those politicians need to get laid with their wives and not some hooker. They shouldn't marry an undesirable woman in the first place if they don't want to fuck her. Whatever their definition of undesirable is. And as for pop stars, well that's a whole different story."

"Sexual frustration causes war. Hahaha!" She laughed out loud.

"True 'Dat!" I blurted.

George had overheard our conversation and just gazed at us. I sometimes forget he was from the South. Serenity blushed, so did I.

"What? You think us Southerners don't have a knack for sexual anecdotes? I bought three of those books. I live in the city and play drums in a band so would both of you stop looking at me like that? You don't have to put the girl talk on lockdown because I'm here." He smiled and continued "I think those pop stars should try some butter, that way they wouldn't be so hungry all the time and wind up divorcing their husbands for no reason. Or maybe they should start cooking with butter so their husbands wouldn't leave them!"

We all giggled. George was right, butter was the secret ingredient to many things. "See, that's why I hired this guy. He enjoys butter as much as I do. We never fight because we're rarely hungry." Serenity had fired an employee two months after she opened because the bitch wanted to put me and Serenity on a diet. Mind you, we both were not in any way obese. She ate cardboard with pigeon-crap that she said was tofu. Her name was Barbara. Serenity had named her, Bulimic Barbara but then christened Clarabel with that name (after tweaking it) followed by Barbara being fired.

More clients had come in and I went again to the back room in order to do my own tweaking of the journal entries. The computer was still on and everything was running smoothly. I divided the invoices into two stacks and started stapling remittances that were paid. Someone softly knocked on the doorframe. I looked up and it was my musky white rose garden.

"Hey, Polly. Came to pick up some books. Serenity told me that you were back here doing some accounting. You didn't strike me as an accountant."

"Well, that was my livelihood once. It was like joining the convent only, I didn't find my calling." I grinned.

"Oh, I wasn't talking about that, it's just you look too alive to be one. You're interesting." He grinned back.

"Like I said, didn't find my calling." I smiled. Ok, I was trying to be less of a cold fish.

"But you made a tremendous career leap from accountant to undertaker."

"And you made a tremendous leap from Betty Crocker to Undercover Brother."

"Very funny. I hope you didn't suffer from a big hangover the next day."

"Yes, at the beginning. I usually can hold my liquor better than this. I'm really sorry you had to see that."

"Well, to be fair you were out of practice and you had too many tequila shots in between drinks. But man, you can drink."

"Little jealous, aren't we?"

"Nope, I can take you on any day."

"You barely had three drinks."

"Well, you know couldn't drink that much, drinking and driving and all that."

"Yeah. I usually call a cab and just leave my car parked. It's something my dad taught my sister and I when we started drinking. No matter what, he or mom would either pick us up or send us a cab or give us extra money for one."

"Sounds like your dad is very responsible and understanding. He understands that you are entitled to a buzz and having good time yet being responsible."

"Yeah, he never judges. I rarely keep secrets from him. He's the most understanding person. He has a wicked sense of humor."

"I could see where you got that from. Anyhow, I think I must leave now since you're busy. I really enjoyed my five second dance with you at Serenity's birthday."

I narrowed my eyes. "You're welcome. By the way, you forgot you scarf at my place when you dropped me off."

"Oh yeah, that." He nodded his head slowly. "I meant to leave that there for you."

"Why on Earth would you do that?" I asked but then it hit me right away. Before he could answer I carried on; "Mr. Black, if you think leaving your scarf on purpose at my house will give you a chance to see me again, then you're wrong. I would appreciate it if you'd stop this cocky charade of yours. It's mind-numbingly stupid and just pure boorish. I have no intention of having any relations with you or any homosapien with two ding-dongs whatsoever."

"Polly, stop going all thesaurus on me! Never knew I could bring out the Merriam Webster in you. Would you please stop attacking me like that? Yeah, so what if I want to see you again? I find you very interesting and I am very fond of your brains and excessive use of perfect grammar and vocabulary when you get nervous."

His eyebrows furrowed; "You don't think I feel bad about all that's happened? I meant that very last part in my letter. I never write letters to anyone, well, only to Sandy if I'm going to ditch work. I haven't been able to sleep ever since I shot you by accident. Nothing will ever erase the image of your head falling lifelessly onto my chest while being drenched in your blood. I can still smell your blood on my fingers. When evidence returned my shirt, I didn't wash it. I sleep every night with that shirt next to me, to remind me how I had almost killed an innocent beautiful person who didn't give a second thought about her own well-being. When I found out that Michael dragged you into a bathroom stall to explain his side of his twisted fucked up world, I was sick to my stomach. The first thing I asked Eddie if he had hurt you. I will catch him if it is the last thing I do. He hurt you so badly that you can't bear to trust anyone."

My eyes were misty. He was mad as hell, but he wasn't done. *Man, was he a talker.* "Yeah, I read your file and his file. You saved up money to go watch him on opening night no matter what country he was in. You were the best thing that ever happened to him. You were a true friend and if that KGB bastard had played his cards right, he would have had you- instead; he chose a career with his girlfriend as the Russian version of Bonnie and Clyde, only they didn't want to kill half of the fuckin population to prove a point. Sick bastard."

He looked at me with his piercing green eyes. I thought he was going to drill a hole into my forehead with them. My tears were smashing onto the invoices on the table. I didn't cry or make sniffle sounds. It was just my tear ducts had diarrhea. And there it was that knot at the back of my throat. My chest tightened and I couldn't breathe, but I kept my cool. I didn't want to lose it in front of him. I never tend to give any ding-dong the pleasure of victory. I became sweaty and nervous. Serenity was calling me from outside; she probably had ordered Chinese. I ignored her call.

"In a minute, we're discussing something about the case." He shouted.

"No problem, take your time guys. I'm not going back, close the door if you need privacy." *Damn you Serenity.*

Castor closed the door. I knew he wanted to continue his lecture, but I couldn't go on listening. I stood up abruptly and wiped my tears with my sleeve. He stood in front of me to block my way. He proceeded to move closer to me and I put my fist against his chest and lightly pushed him back. He removed my fist and opened it. His hands were cold.

He then put it over his heart. I could feel his chest was as hard as the tombstones Angelo made. His heart was beating fast.

His eyes never left mine. He then tilted toward me and kissed me at the corner of my mouth. I was paralyzed for a second. He wanted me to reciprocate and I did.

I delivered a left hook to his jaw. He lost balance a bit but recovered fast. He rubbed his jaw. He moved from my way and I told him before leaving the room: "Like I said, stop this cocky charade of yours. By the way, it's never polite to kiss a lady without her permission or they don't teach you that in FBI school?" I left the room and slammed the door behind me. I slid to the floor and sobbed silently.

14

Serenity and George were having a debate on whether Yun Dun was Mandarin word for dumplings. When she saw me enter the front room, she got up and turned to George.

"George, please lock the front door." She demanded softly.

"Sure thing." He got up and locked the front door and turned the sign post to 'Closed'.

She turned back to me and held my chin up. She was examining my face and it was embarrassing. She automatically hugged me. And I broke down in sobbing spasms.

"Honey, what's wrong?" She removed a matted tendril from my sweaty face.

"He lectured me then kissed me on the corner of my mouth. I punched him and left the room." *Oh, fuck my life I need to stop sobbing. What is wrong with me? Big girls don't cry. I had a mental image of myself eye-rolling, well, myself.*

"If I'd known that you were going to hurt Castor I would've dragged you myself here." I could hear the grin in her voice.

"Hurt him? He was awful to me. He hurt my feelings. He's still in the back and I don't want to see him ever again." I said in a low tone.

Castor had just entered the front room. I could see that he was not happy at all and he looked a bit guilty. Serenity disengaged from me and stood back. Castor didn't move his eyes from me. He then greeted Serenity and George with a nod. George unlocked the front door and let him out. As George opened the door, a dusk of wind blew at him and his scent, again, filled my nostrils. I may need professional help after this. As George was locking the front door again, he said: "Polly, do you mind if I say something?"

"No." I said.

"A guy should never kiss a girl without her permission. But Castor doesn't need your permission." I could not believe he was saying this with a straight face.

Serenity jumped in and said: "George, what are you talking about? Does he think antagonizing her then trying to kiss her is going to work? Who does he think he is? I like Castor but I draw the line when it's my friend he's hurting."

"Serenity, I watched Castor during your birthday party. His expression turns glum when she leaves his side. I watched him all night. Your friends, Dana and Alan thought that Polly and Castor were an item at times." He said a matter-of-factly.

"George, he thinks we have this connection, but we don't. He was just being annoying. He practically followed me around that evening because it's his job and it is his case. The FBI are still looking for Michael." I explained.

"I see. I didn't know that he was still pursuing your case. My apologies. Dumpling?"

Yeah, Georgie...let's deflect.

"Yes, please." I smiled.

It was already 9 p.m. and George had left. I finished up some invoices for Serenity and she was boxing some books. I came up front and cleared out the counter for her.

"What did he tell you that caused you to cry like that? I know you well, you almost never cry at movies. The only time I ever saw you cry this way was at your mom's funeral. What could he have said to you that made you cry like this?" she sounded miffed. I told her the whole thing from A to Z.

"Oh my God, he sleeps next to his shirt that was drenched in your blood? That's romantically morbid. *And* I told you that it wasn't just me who thought that Michael was in love with you; even Agent Hottie sees it."

"He was just theorizing, Serenity. But you're right he's

hot." I snorted.

"If he's hot then what's your problem? I don't go around delivering punches to guys who like me."

I have no idea what's my fuckin problem. Maybe my mother dropped me on my head as a baby.

"It's not as simple as you think. He's too intense for me." *Intense*- that was the word I was looking for. I disliked anything *intense* albeit I loved blood and gore.

"Intense? You mean too passionate for you. The guy made you feel his heart. How did his chest feel? Just wondering..." She grinned and shook her shoulder jokingly.

"It was tombstone hard. The shape of his chest reminded me of a tombstone Angelo once made for this family and.." she cut me off mid-sentence.

"Normal people associate hard chests with stones, you, on the other hand, associate them with tombstones and boulders. You're perfect for each other, he sleeps with your blood and you think of tombstones when you feel his chest. You're both quirky."

"Please, you did not just say that."

"I did."

That evening I left Serenity's shop feeling utterly confused. I still had the same CD in the player. I started fantasizing about Castor. The way his soft lips touched the corner of my mouth. The way he held my hand against his heart. I didn't want to give in to him. I just wasn't in that place in my life now. I didn't want a relationship with anyone.

Two days had passed and no sign of Castor. I had been going to Serenity's daily to fix some of the journals on her system after my shifts. I was also training George how to create barcodes. I didn't see Castor either, although, he had left his stack of books there. He paid for them but never took them with him. I was reluctant to give them to him myself, but I chose not to. I didn't tell my father about my incident with Castor, though I did tell Anne. She said that I'd see things in due time. If I wasn't ready, then I wasn't ready. My dad was having the guys over tonight. I had promised to help him. Anne was bringing some of her friends over as well. I had just awakened after my one-hour nap. I had been so tired that day from digging all those plots with Elijah. I heard voices downstairs and assumed that Uncle James and my dad were talking.

But there were more than two voices. I heard yelling and thudding. It didn't sound like horseplay. It sounded serious. I was very much half-asleep. I presumed the worst. I searched my closet and got out Michael's baseball bat. I ran downstairs only to find my father tackling somebody. I didn't know where I got the strength from, but I jumped over the banister and landed on the back of whoever my father was trying to tackle. He landed on the floor face down. I clobbered him a few times then threw the useless baseball bat aside and started kicking him. I heard everyone screaming and yelling. My father was trying to pry me off the guy.

"Polly, stop it! We're just horsing around! Stop clobbering him! Jesus, are you on anabolic steroids. Please, stop!" Another set of hands grabbed me.

He and Uncle James finally pried me off him. I saw Francis Prique and Eddie Ball help my prey off the floor. He was bleeding and I couldn't see his face. They put him on the couch, and it was Castor Black. I looked at my father in horror and yelled at him.

"What the hell is he doing in our house!?" I was trying to catch my breath.

"Polly, calm down! What has gotten into you?" He went on in a softer tone: "I invited Castor and I thought that I should invite the guys at the headquarters and Eddie with Uncle James for dinner. Sandy is unloading the van. Castor was showing me some hand to hand combat. We were just horsing around, that's all. I'm sorry to have scared you like this sweetheart. I'm so sorry." He came up and gave me a big bear hug.

"I'm sorry dad, I thought that the Russian mob was coming to kill us." That fuckin lump in my throat. *It had better be nodules.*

"No, sweetie. But I think we need to take Castor to the

hospital."

I looked at Castor with revulsion and saw the blood oozing from the back of his head to his neck and chest. Vince was applying pressure on his wounds. I ordered the *prick and ball* to take Castor to my car. I wanted to drive him to the hospital. I ran upstairs and threw on the clothes I had been wearing that day. I rushed downstairs and they had put Castor next to the driver's seat. I reached over him to put on his seatbelt thus brushing against him. I could hear him panting. I put my car in overdrive and sped down the street to the hospital. Sandy was in front of his van holding a tray of food staring at us dumbfounded.

"I don't want you speeding, and Sandy could've taken me to the hospital." He said laboriously.

"It's ok. I'm so sorry, I would have never imagined it was you or anybody horsing around at my house that way. You're going to be ok."

We didn't say another word after that. He closed his eyes. I could tell that he was in pain. I reached the emergency entrance of the hospital and someone came with a wheelchair to assist Castor. He preferred to walk. So, he walked in with the aid of a medic. Half an hour later, Sandy met me in the waiting room.

"Polly, is it true? Did you clobber my brother?" His eyes were wide with disbelief.

"Yes, but only because I thought someone had broken into my house and attacked my dad. I had just woken up." I looked at him sheepishly.

"Boy, I never saw Castor get beat up by a girl or anyone-and twice in one week. You deliver one heck of a left hook. I had to put a steak on his face that evening. Don't worry he'll be fine. I just came here to give you his wallet. He forgot it at your place. You and he meet me back there and I'll take him home."

"Alright." I said and he patted me on the shoulder.

Two hours later and Castor walked out with four stitches on the back of his head. The ER doctor told me that he didn't have any swelling but I shouldn't let him fall asleep for another eight hours. The doctor was smiling a bit too much. I filled out his paper work and we left. I helped him into the car and buckled him up. I went to sit in the driver's seat. I started the car.

"Are you alright?" I was deeply concerned.

"Yes, this is nothing. Please don't worry. It's not my first clobbering. Could you please take me home?"

"But your brother said to bring you back to my house."

"Alright, whatever." He said sharply.

"Are you in pain?"

"No, actually I can't feel a thing."

"They gave you a shot that's why maybe."

"No, I didn't let them give me a shot. There are other things more mind-numbing than pain." He managed a faint smile.

'*Like Stupidity*' I answered him in my head. He was still hurting. I made believe that I hadn't understood his comment. It was a very quiet drive back to my house. We stopped at a red light. It started to rain a bit. He put on my CD player and I noticed a moment too late that I hadn't changed the CD. He sighed then shut it off. We reached my place and he unbuckled himself and walked straight to the backdoor. I followed him inside. Anne was in the kitchen with her friends discussing a trip to Paris. She motioned with her finger to Castor asking what happened. I held up my hand meaning that I'd explain later.

Castor told Sandy and my dad that he wasn't allowed to sleep for eight hours because of his minor concussion. My dad managed a light snort. "Well, we can keep you up for the first 4 or 5 hours but the rest you can do at home." My father said to Castor. He then fixed him a plate of buffalo wings and celery. Castor plopped himself on the couch next to me. He opened a can of cold beer.

"I don't think you should be drinking." I advised.

"This isn't the first time I get stitches." He derided.

"Alright, put yourself in a coma for all I care."

He grabbed my hand as I was trying to get up. “Have a beer.” He offered. I took the can and opened it. I guzzled almost half the can while breathing through my nose. “I’m impressed.” He said. “I wasn’t trying to, I was just thirsty.” I grinned and got up. I was planning on enjoying my beer in peace. I took my half of can of beer and went to the kitchen and asked one of Anne’s friends for a cigarette. I lit it and headed to the backyard. It had been since my mom passed that I sat next to her hydrangeas. Michael was the one who planted them for her. She preferred lilies but let Michael have his own little bushel in our backyard.

Why did I get so depressed whenever I remembered Michael? I know it’s normal, but it was the type of depression that caused me to feel drowsy and sleepy. Half an hour later of much needed disheartening contemplation, I finished my beer and went around the house to go upstairs. I didn’t feel like talking to anyone. I didn’t even look for Castor. I didn’t bother turning on the light in my bedroom. I just kicked off my shoes and took off my pants. I didn’t bother to brush my teeth. I got under the covers and searched for my other pillow to snuggle with, instead I found a lump of someone next to me. From his smell, I knew it was Castor. He was sleeping deep. My dad must’ve told him he could crash in the guest room but he probably ‘got lost’ and found his way to my room. I wore my pants again and went downstairs to tell my dad that Castor was sleeping in my bed.

“Yeah, I was looking for you. But I told him to sleep in the guest room for a while, he seemed very tired. Poor guy must’ve gotten confused. But he shouldn’t be sleeping.”

“Look, I don’t care. I’m going to crash in the guest room. You must wake him up in a while. I have a very early shift at work tomorrow.” There was no way in hell I was going to take care of him. I had a little too much Castor for one week. Bastard was like a hemorrhoid.

“Alright, Polly; good night.” He kissed me on the cheek.

I went upstairs to the guest room. It took me a few minutes to remove all the pillows from the bed. I locked the door behind me because I didn’t want to have any midnight surprises. I took off my pants and threw myself on the bed. I could've opened the closet and worn pajamas. My mom had the best guest room, whatever you needed you'd find. With that thought, I snuggled a pillow and drifted off to Lala Land.

The next morning, I woke up real early. I could hear my father downstairs making breakfast. I snuck into my room and no Castor. But my bathroom door was shut, and I could hear the shower inside. I opened my closet fast and grabbed fresh underwear, socks and a bra. I opened another closet and nicked out a pair of pants and a t-shirt. I didn't have time to look for a sweater, so I just grabbed the nearest cardigan. I rushed back to the guest room and decided to take advantage of the toiletries in the guest bathroom. I took a quick shower, but I didn't wash my hair. I wanted to get out of the house before Castor left. I got dressed in a jiffy. I went back into my bedroom to grab my messenger bag for work. I heard the shower go off; I ran in and took the bag and dashed downstairs. *Yeah, I'm childish. I know.*

"Good morning Sunshine. Castor spent the night here."

"Yeah, I noticed the lump on my bed."

"Sorry, but Sandy didn't want to wake him up. I woke him up and he stayed up for almost 2 hours and went back to bed. That guy really knows how to sleep off a concussion. He's taking a shower and I had to give him fresh towels from the linen closet in the hallway. Your door was locked."

"Yeah, I preferred to lock it. You know, a strange guy sleeping in the house."

"Polly, you clobbered an FBI agent; I don't think he'd be getting any ideas soon and if he had, I think you've made yourself clear."

Yeah, that's what my dad thinks. How was I going to tell him that Castor was on a personal vendetta to be the world's biggest asshole – hemorrhoids and all? I grabbed my grilled cheese sandwich and headed to my car. I turned on the engine and changed the CD in my player. I didn't want to feel anything this morning but the cold. The roads were slippery, and I could barely see from all the fog. I finally reached the parlor. I saw Marc getting out of his car and heard him yelling all sorts of profanities at his umbrella. I told him no matter how expensive, the wind would ravage them. I ran up to him and we both took shelter under my massive umbrella. We made it to the entrance just before it started pouring heavily. Uncle James didn't look like he was in a good mood. Marc and I greeted him and went on our way.

"I think the receptionist screwed up again." Marc whispered.

"Why do you say that?"

"She keeps leaving the front desk when she shouldn't. You know how many phone calls we've been getting lately from new customers?"

"Yeah, so? Isn't that good?"

"Yeah, that's not the point. She is always on her cell outside. To make matters worse, some new customers tend to trash our competitors over the phone or when they come by us and she shouldn't reciprocate. This isn't Yelp. She is a serial gossiper. She thinks she has her own talk show."

"Oh, man. Uncle James may give her the pink slip without a warning. That man hates to gossip especially about other competitors. Now, they'll think we're dishing dirt about them when it's been her the whole time. Angelo mentioned to me that Homer's Home were going to sue Uncle James for defamation if we didn't stop the rumors."

"Well, Mr. Roberts found out last week that it was her. But he decided to give her a second chance and made her apologize to Mr. Homer personally."

"What could she have possibly said that made Mr. Homer so angry?"

"She went around confirming to clients that he indeed had a necrophile working with the corpses."

"Are you serious?" *Jeez, does anyone have any professional courtesy anymore?*

"As a heart attack. Now, it's true what she's saying, and I know it but we don't respond to clients when they ask. We just simply claim that we don't appreciate talking about our friendly business colleagues."

"I hope he fires her. Uncle James has just begun expanding the business. We don't need a lawsuit. I'll talk to him later."

"Yeah, I think you should."

I saw Angelo polishing the marble tombstone for our 4p.m. funeral. I had been working with him all day. Elijah had received most of the orders. He was a hard worker. I was notified later during the day that the priest wasn't going to make it. We had two chaplains at the home, but I knew the family wouldn't agree because they were Catholic. I gave Father Arella a call. He was very happy to come on such short notice. He was one of the few Catholic priests who really cared about his flock. We were very well established with him. He is great friends with Uncle James.

I went to talk to Uncle James to assure him that everything was on track.

"Uncle James, I took care of everything for the Keenan's funeral at 4. I'm heading to the embalming room. Do you need me to do anything else?"

"No, Polly. Thank you. What time is Father Arella coming?"

"He'll be here at 3. Is everything alright with you?"

"Yes, I'm alright now because I fired the receptionist. I called Mr. Homer and explained to him the situation. We made nice and I told Tippy from HR to give a friendly informal heads-up to Pepino's Funeral Home. I don't want to get on Sal Pepino's bad side in any way."

"Wow." I mouthed.

"Yeah, I know. Go now, Marc's probably wondering which type of lipstick he should use for Mrs. Keenan." He smiled.

I walked down the hall to the embalming room. It was already 2p.m. and I didn't have my lunch break. I was too nervous to eat. I still hadn't digested this morning's grilled cheese sandwich. I didn't know why I was so tense today. I could still feel Castor's heartbeat on my hand. I could still feel his light kiss on the corner of my mouth, so soft, so erroneous. I walked faster to the embalming room because I didn't want to be alone with my brain any longer. I reached the room and Marc was in dilemma not about the lipstick though but whether if her dress was making her look too fat.

"For real?" I raised my eyebrows.

"Well, it makes her look fat. The worst thing I can do is make a woman look bad at her own funeral."

"It's her funeral not wedding, Marc."

"I have a reputation to sustain. I'm serious. Can you help me, please?"

"Sure." Dressing a dead lady sounded much better than being alone with my brain.

Ten minutes later, we were done. She wasn't that stiff. Marc was looking at the corpse as if Da Vinci were admiring one of his creations. He brushed her hair and added more hairspray.

"I think the nude lipstick would look better on her. She's too tanned."

"You're right, what did she die of? skin cancer? Her skin is so leathery and dry. She hasn't been dead for 48 hours, right?"

"She died in her sleep. Brain aneurysm."

"I never understood that type of COD." I huffed.

"Me too. I think she's been dead for twenty hours. Thanks for helping me. How are you getting along with Elijah?"

"He's alright. He's picking up fast and that's what I want."

"Can I tell you something but keep it between us?"

"Oh, thank you, I'm dying for some gossip." I pleaded happily.

"Elijah asked me yesterday if you were seeing someone. I think he's interested." He whispered.

"What did you tell him?"

"Well, I told him that I didn't know because I really, umm, didn't know."

"I'm not involved with anybody but tell him that I am. I don't want to stir up relationships at work and he's not my type at all. I'm not interested in him whatsoever. So, if he or anybody asks you anything like that tell them I'm with someone."

"I understand. I don't blame you. But for real, Polly, I've been here with you for almost two years and I have never seen you go out with anyone."

"Well, last year was pretty hectic and I had just broken up with my boyfriend and this year, like you know, my mom died, my childhood friend's a terrorist and you know the rest of the gory details."

"A little birdy told me that you went to Serenity's birthday with a hottie."

"The little birdy being Anne; Oh him, he was just escorting me. Serenity's employee couldn't pick me up that day. And that 'hottie' was the guy who shot me."

Marc's jaw dropped. "You went to Serenity's birthday with Castor Black?"

"Yes, so what? She sent him to me, and I had no choice but to go with him." I huffed and puffed. "Please don't tell me that he's your neighbor or dog walker or mortuary supplies retailer."

"Oh, no. But Anne showed me a picture of him, and that guy is too hot to be an FBI agent. Anne filled me in on the details."

"Marc, if you want to date him, I can make it happen for you. And stop discussing my personal life with my sister."

"Honey, I'm straight as a line and I can't help but gossip with Anne when I go for my monthly pick-up for clothes. Why don't you date him, seriously?"

"He's not my type. My sister thinks I like him, but I don't. He was undercover whilst the whole Michael fiasco and I got caught up in the middle."

"Have it your way but you want to know what I think?"

"Please before you may have an aneurysm yourself from all the theorizing."

"I'm serious Polly, your friendship with Michael has messed you up. Here you had a person who you knew would never hurt you, but he managed to in some way. Now, he's missing, and you still don't understand why he became this way. You never got your closure from him."

"Marc, I was never romantically involved with him. He was my childhood friend and one of my best friends. I would have taken a bullet for him. I never had any romantic feelings for him. I promise."

"Oh, I understand that. It's just that during the events before your shooting, Anne told me about the jacket. It was like someone brought to your attention that he loves you. You didn't accept it and even if you tried, he'd already hurt you."

"I'm not following."

"See, when I told you that Elijah was interested in you, your brain like any other, will try to have a romantic image of yourself and him; either accepting or rejecting the idea, but you automatically rejected it. It's normal human behavior. You can't tell me that your brain didn't picture you and Michael for just a split second. I mean, he's familiar territory, easy-going, comfortable and he knows all your vices."

"I've never thought of it that way. Let's say you're right for a moment, how can I get closure from someone who is missing?"

"All you have to do is move on. It's difficult and I know that, but Anne really thinks that you feel something for Agent Hottie. She told me you clobbered him and took him to the emergency room. Your sister is worried about you but is too afraid to even broach the subject with you. Could you just try at least? I don't think he can do any more damage than he's already done. He's doing everything backwards; he gave you a hole in your chest, you went out, he tried to kiss you, you smacked him, then clobbered him. So, if you put these events backwards, you have yourself a normal relationship." He laughed.

"Yeah, backwards." I laughed. I couldn't help but resent the fact that everyone around me is psychoanalyzing me. *Has everyone minored in shrinkery whilst I was in a coma?*

The funeral service went as planned. Uncle James was very happy with the work we did. I made sure everything ran smooth, I didn't want to see him in the same mood as this morning. My shift was almost over, and I didn't want to go home. My bed was going to smell like him. Well, I could always cremate the mattress and sheets in the parlor's crematorium.

An hour later and I was home, I ran upstairs to do some damage control. I had purchased Clorox for colors because my sheets were gray and black. My room was an utter mess. I stripped my mattress and pillows. I put them in a pile on the floor with the pillows. I went to the bathroom and removed all the towels he used and the ones he might've used plus the bathrobe I assumed he'd worn. I dumped those on the pile and scanned my bedroom for anything else he might've used and ran downstairs with my mountain of linen to the laundry room. I put the washing machine on the soiled cycle and pour in 2 cups of Clorox. I poured 2 caps of fabric softener. I felt relieved. I ran upstairs again and sprinkled my mattress with baking soda. My mom had told me once that baking soda absorbs the bad odors, but she never said anything about the good intoxicating ones. I let the baking soda settle for a while.

I went downstairs to fix dinner. I haven't done that in a long time. I opened the fridge and of course there were steaks, but I decided that we needed an evening of food sans meat. I needed to go to the supermarket. I gave Anne a call to see what she wanted to eat.

"Hullo? Polly is that you?"

"Yeah, what did your caller ID say?"

"Very funny. Are you ok?"

"Yeah, I'm going to fix dinner tonight and wondered what you would like to eat. I'm heading out the door to the supermarket." I put my coat on as I was trying to press the phone between my ear and shoulder.

"Actually, I was going to make ricotta and spinach ravioli. Sandy prepared the dough before coming by us yesterday. He was going to make it for us till you decided to make marinara sauce out of Castor's brains. Anyways, all you should do is cut the squares and stuff them with ricotta and spinach, top it with marinara and parmesan."

"Yeah, I know how to make it. I taught you, remember?"

"I know. Did you see Castor this morning?"

"No, I left early."

"Yeah, I saw that." I could hear her smiling.

"If you saw that, why are you asking me?"

"Just making sure I was right. Would you please stop avoiding him?"

"I'm not avoiding him. I had to be at work early and would you please stop discussing my love life with Marc?"

"Why would I discuss something with Marc that doesn't exist? Also, Marc is very friendly, and we discuss about current events sometimes."

"I'm going to shut the phone before I reach into the receiver to strangle you. I have to leave. Now, MYOB."

"Alright, see you in an hour or so."

As I reached the car, I hung up on my sister with a goodbye. I put my cell phone on the passenger's seat. I just remembered that I didn't find Castor's scarf when I was stripping my bed. He must've taken it. If not, it'll show up and I'll probably give it to my dad to give it to one of the guys at the headquarters. I put my car in drive and turned on my CD player. I remembered not putting another one into it. A sudden shiver went down my spine and my lips quivered. I felt my heart drop into my boot. It was a Gustav Mahler composition playing on my stereo. I drove as though I've noticed nothing, yet I felt his hand cover my mouth and I almost screamed. I looked through the visor mirror and all I could see was the faint mole on his stiff upper lip.

15

I must stop day dreaming. Maybe I put the CD unconsciously while driving. But no, the imaginary hand felt real and cold. The imaginary stiff upper lip was materializing. I kept on driving, but I was still frozen. I kept telling myself that this wasn't happening, that my intellect was probably diminishing in some way.

"Polly, it's me. Please don't scream. I'm real you're not day dreaming." Those were the words that triggered my tears. He didn't remove his hand from my mouth till he felt the tears on his hand. He moved his hand up and wiped them tenderly from my face. He felt like the Michael I knew during that moment.

"I need you to drive us somewhere where nobody will recognize me. I need to talk to you. I need your help."

"I won't help you. Please leave me alone. I don't want any trouble." I sobbed.

"Listen Polly, you're going to help me because you're not a bitch. So, save us some time about deciding whether you will help because eventually you will help me. You could never live with yourself if you left me stranded. I know you too well."

"I'm not helping a terrorist."

"I'm Michael -not a terrorist." He said through his teeth.

"Well, they've updated the thesaurus. Please get out of my car now."

"I will not." He put something cold to my head and cocked it.

"So, you've come prepared this time so I wouldn't kick you in the balls? I'm not afraid of you or your shitty gun so put that down. If you want to kill me please, be my guest." I was no longer afraid of dying. I wanted my misery to be over.

"You think I won't do it, Polly?"

"Oh, I know you'd do it but I'm just giving you permission to speed the process. At least when you shoot me in the head, I'd die right away. I won't have to go through the agony of surgeries and the countless hours of physical therapy."

"I know, I was there. So just shut up and do as I say!"

"No." I stood my ground.

"Don't make me hurt you. Stop being stubborn."

"No." I drove past the supermarket. I didn't stop.

"I have some cash on me and you're going to rent me a motel room for the night. You're going to make believe we're together."

Really, misery does love company? Ok.

"Are you nuts? Mostly everyone in this area knows me. I'm the only female undertaker around here."

"I know a place where I'm sure no one knows you or me."

"Where?"

Thirty minutes and many directions later, we reached an inn. He got out of the car first and opened my door. I told him that I would leave and drive away as if nothing happened, he refused.

"I need you here with me. Come on, keep me company. Like old times." He smiled faintly. I could see the weariness in his eyes.

"Michael, this isn't a good idea and my sister is going to suspect something's wrong. My father will be home soon."

"Don't worry, I'm not asking you to spend the night just come in have a cup of joe and leave."

I let him have his way. I wanted to know what was going on with him. Maybe that was going to be my closure. Things were never complicated with Michael, this shouldn't be any different. *Have a cup of coffee with the terrorist and leave. It wasn't that complicated.*

We reached the front desk and there was a man in his mid-forties watching the 8'oclock news on a mini screen. My father and Anne should be arriving home almost at the same time. They'll probably assume that I was held up at the supermarket since it was raining cats and dogs. I asked the man for a room for two. I didn't want him to be suspicious that I wasn't spending the night there. Michael had his arm wrapped around my waist as if he were my lover. For some sick reason, I felt warm because I felt comfortable with him. Marc was right.

I handed the man the money and he gave me a keycard. We walked to the room through a dim hallway. When we reached the room, I heard Michael cock his gun. He gave his back to mine just in case someone was following us. I swiped the card and opened the door. I walked in with his back still to mine. *What was going on?* He closed the door and took the keycard from me and locked the door behind us. He didn't let me turn on the lights at first. He took me by my hand and sat me on the bed. He picked up the phone and ordered two cups of coffee, one black for me the way I liked it. He turned on the lights and dimmed them.

I saw his face. His eyes were fatigued, and he had a scar on his forehead. His non-existent hazel eyes looked like the ones of a somnolent child; only they were blue now, he was wearing contacts. His charcoal black hair was now blonde and longer. His makeover brought out his Russian facial features. He was already white but looked too white now. I noticed that he had scars and bruises on his arms. He looked a bit thinner. I heard a light knock on the door, and it was room service. He got up and opened the door. He closed the door with our coffees. He handed me a cup and I just stared at the black liquid.

"What do you want from me?" still staring at the cup.

"Just to be with you."

"I don't want to be with you in the same room. Was me punching you too subtle?"

"I understand that you can't even look at me. I just needed to see you. Look, I put my gun away." He un-cocked his gun and put it on the nightstand.

"Michael, why are you doing this to me? First you kidnap me at gun point now you just want to have coffee with me."

"Well, I had to be prepared. You're nuts, Polly."

"Nuts? You kill people God damn it! You dragged me into a stall like some bully who wanted to give me a swirly."

"I just didn't want you to get anxious and scream. On another note, we were the bullies who gave the other bullies swirlies."

"Well, it was fun. Don't change the subject!" I shook my head.

"Polly, I have a problem."

"Yeah, I know with the FBI."

"The FBI are the least of my worries."

"What then?" I took a sip from my coffee.

"When you said that I was dead to you, I couldn't sleep that night. I couldn't think clear for many days. To make a long story short, Clarabel's father took a trip to Moscow and he was killed by his rival. It was all over the newspapers in Russia. His cell fell disbanded. Some of his men formed their own cells and I decided that I didn't want my dead body to end up strewn across some street in Moscow's ghettos. I've accumulated enough money and assets to last me for a very long time. I'm not greedy and don't want anymore."

"It is said that her father murdered yours?" I blurted.

"Rumors."

"Are you sure?"

"That's not the point." His face was straight

"Then, why are you telling me this?"

"I've hired a very good lawyer and I have evidence for the FBI. They don't have solid evidence against me and never will. You know how we Russians impale everything. We neither deny or admit to anything."

"I see. So, you've got yourself settled then."

"Not quite, I broke up with Clarabel because I found out that she had been cheating on me with this dude Nicolas. He was basically her father's right hand. He formed a new cell with her. I refused to be a part of it. I disappeared and I know their next target and I can't tell you. I have solid evidence and you have to get one of your dad's friends at the police headquarters or the FBI to listen to me."

"I have a better idea."

"Really? What?"

"Remember the guy who shot me on the bus? The undercover agent?"

"Yes, the dude with the long hair. Didn't they jail him?"

"No, I dropped the charges against him. I pretty much got to know him. How about we talk to him? He's the one working on your case after all. He's FBI."

"You what? Are you out of your mind?! He almost killed you but...wait...Well, I shouldn't be surprised. To be fair that bastard meant to shoot me, and you got in the way. That's a good idea but you think he'd listen?"

"Look, he owes me a favor. We kind of have this weird relationship."

"Oh, I see. you're dating him?" His forehead creased.

"No, silly. I said 'relationship' because I can't label it anything. He's trying to be my friend and I kind of refuse his friendly gestures. I think he just feels very bad, that's all."

Michael took two sips from his cup of coffee and placed it on the nightstand. He lay down on the bed and pulled my arm toward him. I was now lying next to him. He held me close to his chest. He ran his fingers through my hair. He had one arm under my head, and we were both staring at the ceiling. I turned to look at his face and I could see a tear running down his temple. Why won't he tell me what is going on exactly? Why the charades and secrecy?

"I never got to kill anyone to be honest. The only charge I'm facing is aiding and abetting terrorists, your FBI friend can't even prove anything because I never trusted him to begin with. It's hard to get something out of a Russian. You know that."

"I know. I've known one practically my whole life. He used to be a ballet dancer and one day he decided that he didn't want a mediocre life."

"I didn't. I'd have mediocrity over terrorism any day. I was going through a bad time that's all. I thought that if I changed my career path, I would be able to have more comfort. Whatever I did, there was always this pang of pain in my soul. Don't ever think that you're mediocre in any way Polly Deuce. Saying that I was dead to you was like someone chopping off my toes one by one without anesthesia; a ballet performer's worst nightmare. I came back for you, don't you understand?"

"For me? Don't put that kind of weight on me, man. You may go to jail."

"For a couple of years maybe. My lawyer's a pig like most of them. Besides, the FBI doesn't have solid evidence against me. I just want this piece of evidence to reach them." He took a small USB stick out of his pocket and put it on my abdomen. I sat up and put it in my trench's inside pocket and patted it.

"I'm going to go to call Castor. I'll reach some compromise. I won't tell him that you gave it to me, and I won't tell him that you didn't." I smiled.

He sat up and hugged me. "Spoke like a true Russian." He kissed me on the cheek. I could hear his breathing getting a bit heavy. He muttered something unintelligible in Russian – I thought.

"What?"

"I said that I love you so much in Russian." He smiled.

"Oh, okay. I'll go now."

"You still don't get it, do you?"

"Yes, I got it. You said something in Russian that I didn't understand and then you translated." *This was getting weird and sweat was coming out of my ass.*

He took a deep breath and exhaled loudly. "Yes, that's right." He looked the other way and got up to put his cup of coffee on the bar.

"How will I reach you?" I immediately changed the subject.

"You can't. Don't worry, I'll come to you. Make sure no

one suspects a thing. You may never know who's watching."

"Alright and no pointing guns at me this time because shoving a barrel up your ass will be a very painful and gruesome experience for you."

"Yeah, you're right. I'm sorry about that. I should've known better that guns don't work with you as well- you know being self-destructive and all that."

He kissed my forehead and I left the room. I ran through the dim hallway and the reception guy wasn't there. Thank God. I reached my car and checked the backseat because I didn't feel like having any more surprises. It was empty. I got in the car and grabbed my phone where I had last put it, on the passenger's seat next to me. There were five missed calls; four were from home and one was an unfamiliar number. I called home and Anne answered.

"Polly, where the hell are you? I called you like four times. Are you ok? I called Castor a half hour ago, I thought that some Russian mob tried to kill you."

"Anne, I'm ok. I just had to do something.... umm...listen...tell Dad I'm ok. I couldn't go to the supermarket. I have to go. I'll be home later I promise. I have to call Castor."

"Alright, just happy you're ok. Love you, bye."

"Love you." I heard her hang up. I looked at the unfamiliar number and dialed it. I had hoped it was Castor's because Anne had called him.

"Agent Black speaking."

"Castor it's Polly."

"Polly! Where have you been? Me and an agent were about to go looking for you."

"I'm sorry but Anne's got a big imagination. Castor, when can I see you alone?"

"Any time you want. Are you alright?"

"I'm fine. Can you meet up with me now?"

"Yes. Where would you like us to meet?"

"How about Club Thingy?"

"Sure. I'll be there in 15 minutes."

"Okay. You may have to wait a bit longer." I didn't want to tell him that I was more than 15 minutes away.

"I love waiting."

"Ok. Bye."

"Bye."

I locked my doors from inside and made sure the evidence was tucked in my trench. I didn't bother turning on my CD player because I was as nervous as hell. I found an emergency cigarette tucked in the glove compartment. I smoked till my heart's content. I didn't know how I was going to tell Castor all this. But he was an FBI agent, so he was probably used to these situations. I kept replaying the images of Michael in my head. What did he mean that he was back *for me*? I really felt that he tried to make a move on me but contained himself, unlike Castor. Michael was always a gentleman. I never tried imagining myself with Michael as a couple. It just wouldn't have made any sense. It felt dirty and wrong, like incest.

I reached Club Thingy and gave my keys to the valet. I never do that, but I just didn't feel like parking my car tonight. The bouncer removed the velvet rope from the pole that was blocking a long queue. I could hear those girls making bitchy comments. I should start wearing a sign that says "Undertaker". I made my way through the dance floor and Castor wasn't anywhere to be found. I took a left and saw someone sitting at the last booth. I couldn't see a face. I walked up to the booth and followed the scent of white musk like a bloodhound. The stranger had three drinks in front of him. I turned around and walked past him to make sure. He stood up and all I could see were those green 'to die for' eyes. He got out of the booth and made me sit inside and then he sat next to me.

"I didn't know you smoked."

I must really reek.

"Only when I'm anxious or stressed."

He looked surprised.

"Can I have one those drinks with a cigarette later for outside?" The staff knew me.

"Are you anxious or stressed?" He pressed

"Yes."

"Here's your martini." I was handed a pack of cigarettes and a glass of water. The third drink on the table was Castor's drink -presumably.

"Are you sure everything's alright with you?"

"Yes."

"So, you just wanted to see me?" He elbowed my arm jokingly. His smile was so wonderful. His lips curled up in the funniest way when he smiled. I just wanted to rip them off and fry them with some Polish bacon. Very yummy.

I didn't answer his question.

I took a sip from my martini. I mean if I am going to give him this evidence in a concealed manner, I would need alcohol because my courage was on vacay. I took a deep breath and started babbling with him –incessantly.

"Polly, what's going on? You went missing for a couple of hours and you're babbling. Are you ok?"

Not looking at him. "Yes, I just need to give you something and I don't know how. I'm sorry but I don't know how to be all mob-by and FBI-ish."

"I see." He took a sip from his scotch. "Polly where is this something?"

"It's in my trench coat pocket. The inside pocket, left side just adjacent to my chest." *Breast* was the word I needed to say but I just felt weird using that word around him.

I was a bit worried about how I was going to do the transfer and about the third degree of FBI interrogations. He took another sip of his scotch. We sat there for a minute or two without saying a word. He then turned to me and said: "I'm going to have to do something a bit FBI-ish but you have to promise not to be offended or afraid because I'm pretty sure that what you have has something to do with Twinkle Toes."

I couldn't help but feel offended that he had labeled Michael that. Did he have something against men who danced professionally? I didn't answer him. I wasn't up for FBI arrogance.

"Polly, I can tell when someone needs to say something when they can't. It's part of the job. So, let me make this easy for you. You have something from Michael, and you need to give it to me without giving yourself away. Most probably somebody is watching us. You don't need to do anything. Let me do the work. Just go with the flow. Okay? I promise I won't hurt you."

Why would he hurt me? I was confused. As I was running the possibilities of the transfer in my mind. He grabbed me and planted his lips on the hollow of my neck. I could feel his breathing and I went completely numb. I felt his hand slip into my inside pocket, removing the USB stick. He then slid his hand up to my face and planted a light, respectable kiss on my cheek. The intimacy was a bit too much. I was very uncomfortable yet relieved that he had the evidence with him now.

I gazed at him.
He was ogling me with piercing discerning eyes. I just wanted to smack the Adonis out of him.

"What's with the ogling?"

"I'm trying to figure something out."

"I'm not up for any of your schemes, especially not after you violated my personal space like that."

"It was the only way. If you have any problem with my work conduct, you can always send a complaint to my supervisor."

"I hear your supervisor likes you. I don't stand a chance."

"My point exactly. Nevertheless, when is Mr. Nabakov going to turn himself in?"

"Who said anything about that?"

"Polly, it's the same cycle with these cretins. The hunter becomes the hunted and they'd do anything to get themselves out. They bring evidence that 'clears their name' and try to cut a deal with us."

"Michael isn't that type of person."

"I'm sorry to burst your bubble but they all are Ms. Deuce."

"Castor, he won't turn himself in till you see the evidence."

"Honey, I'm not in the FBI because of my rebelliousness." He rolled his eyes. "I actually know a lot about you than you think. I looked you up after I shot you. I never thought about the importance of your role in Nabakov's life, but I was wrong. He never mentioned anything about his childhood."

"Of course, I am and so he is...or was. We were raised together. What are you getting at?"

"Did you open the USB case?"

"Case? It's a stick." *Duh*

"I am pretty sure it is a case masking another stick inside." He explained.

"Of course, I didn't. I promised that I would hand it to you and I never open things that don't concern me. My only goal was to hand over the evidence to you."

I felt sick with apprehension.

"We can't continue this conversation here." He took me by my hand and led me outside.

"Let me walk you to your car." He offered.

"I gave it to valet."

"Give me the card." He ordered.

"Why?"

"Just give it to me please." He took the card from me and held my hand as if we were two teenagers walking out of prom. We reached the sidewalk and he gave my card to the valet guy. I saw him slip the key of his car into the bouncer's pocket. Castor patted him on the back. As we waited for the car, Castor sent a text message to someone. Once my car arrived, he took the keys from the valet guy and sat in the driver's seat. I sat in the passenger's next to him.

"Why did you just give your keys to the bouncer?"

"I can't say."

"Alright, why did you come with me?"

"I can't say." He kept his eyes focused on the road.

"So, this is how it's going to be?"

"No, actually. I have two agents waiting at your house with Lieutenant Francis Prique."

"Why? I didn't break the law!"

"No, you didn't but you have to understand that if you've just seen Michael, which I'm sure of, then Petrov will be watching your house. Clarabel will make sure that her boyfriend's thugs will hurt you because she doesn't like you to begin with. They're just there for protection incase anything goes down."

"How do you know that about her?"

"A birdie told me."

"So, this is how it's going to be?"

"Umm..Polly, Listen carefully... Michael knows that you wouldn't have opened the case; that's how much he knows you. He knows how to manipulate the subordinate in you. He knows that you will never stick your nose in any pie, I'm impressed. I bet that there isn't evidence inside or more likely something else. We're going to the FBI headquarters."

"Well it bodes well for me that you are impressed by my subordination." I said sarcastically. I was in no way a subordinate. *Subordinate my ass*. Where did he minor in shrinkery?

"Bodes well for you? I'm sorry did you acquire the newfangled dictionary of Queen Victoria in the last 15 seconds? What's it with you and the Amish English?"

"I'm sorry. I didn't know that FBI agents were required to fail their SATs in order to get into the academy."

"Ouch! Jesus! You're mean for an accountant. No, we actually get waterboarded while solving word puzzles."

"I almost, almost chuckled." *I really did.*

"Ha! Oh my God. Never knew an accountant with a sense of humor. I think I just gave myself a bone bruise by laughing."

He guffawed and I just kept a straight face. What the hell is happening here?

"I told you before that I'm not an accountant, I used to be one. I'm an undertaker and I swear to Beelzebub that I'll bury you alive."

"Alright, I'm sorry. But you're mean *and funny*. We're about to reach the headquarters. Don't get out of the car till open the door for you." I turned my head away from him.

He was driving a bit too fast. I was getting very uncomfortable. What had gotten into me? Couldn't I have just given it to him in another way? Maybe I just needed a reason to get close to him then withdraw safely. *Summabitch FBI agent, needed a reason to smell him. Alright, I needed professional help.*

We reached the headquarters and two agents escorted me in the building. Castor was behind me. We went up to the office and his supervisor was there. Castor was briefing him about the evidence. They brought in some type of tech geek to open the case and there actually was a USB in there. No surprise there but with Michael, who knows? They brought in another geek to use a special super geek computer to insert the USB. We all stared at the big screen in the office. The geek opened the file and there he was on the screen. *My heart skipped a beat.*

16

There he was on the screen, pre-Russian guise. Michael was speaking fluent Russian-*or that's what it appeared to me.* I had known him for many years and seldom heard him speak more than two sentences in Russian to his mom. He did not have an accent. He spoke English all the time. He used to tell me that his Russian was not that good because he didn't speak it that much and the only Russian, he knew was from his mother prior to meeting Clarabel.

He went on for what seemed like five minutes in Russian. He was a whole different person. I read once that people's personalities changed when they spoke a different language. I get it now.

It was an eerie feeling watching Michael ramble in Russian. He was so taciturn and collected. I guess you never really know someone, do you? It was like me flipping through those European channels my dad had subscribed to once. Castor and his supervisor listened intently. Did they both know Russian as well? I didn't see a translator.

He then said in the end in English; "Castor Black, I've never killed anything by accident. I only used Polly as bait to send this message personally to you. I hope you convey only this part of the message to her."

My mind went completely blank and I could feel my carotid artery was about to erupt. He had used me again and I was the only one to blame. He made me think that he was somehow innocent in some way. I erased the memory of the Michael that I saw two hours ago to the Michael I had seen in the bathroom stall at the clinic. He had me convinced that he had some soft spot for me. I had never felt used in all my life. I didn't want to be all theatrical and melodramatic, especially in front of Castor. *I had to bring out the undertaker in me. Michael was any dead body I was burying. I see this every day. Cry me a river twice and call me Lucille Ball. This was on me.*

"Is everything alright?" Castor asking all concerned, *yeah right.* I scoffed and *almost* chuckled.

"Oh, I'm fine Agent Black. It's just I had never heard Michael speak so fluently in Russian. Just surprised. And the fact that he said that there was evidence showing his innocence. I just don't understand why he would send such incriminating evidence through me."

"That's how these terrorist cells operate sometimes, Polly. Anyways, I need to debrief you in terms of how you acquired this evidence."

"Sure. No problem. Anything you need. May I go to the ladies' room please?"

"Of course, down the hallway." I was escorted by a female agent to the bathroom. She waited outside. I turned on the faucet letting the water run for a few minutes till I could sob no more. I put Lucille Ball to shame. I went back to the office and they had set up a video camera. There was Castor and another agent standing in the room. It was a gruesome hour. He asked me endless questions for my testimony. He was all FBI-ish and I made a mental list of ways to murder Michael Nabakov. I just answered whatever he asked. I left out the part where Michael said that he loved me. I felt it was too personal and irrelevant.

After recording the debrief, I told Castor that I wanted to drive myself home. I didn't want to be near him, let alone any guy. I was done. I just wanted to go home and curl into bed and go to work the next day. He refused to let me go home under strict instructions from his supervisor.

I was advised to have an escort the whole time because they were sure that I was in some sort of danger from Michael. *Man, I can't even seem to bring myself to use the words 'danger' and 'Michael' in the same phrase.* We left the headquarters and Castor drove my car home. He phoned Lieutenant Prique and told him to set shop for him at my house.

"I'm so sorry you had to hear that." He furrowed his brows looking at me.

"Why would you be sorry?" I turned my face away to the window losing myself in the city lights.

"Well, because I know how much you love Michael and you're probably hurt because he hoodwinked you."

Now, who is using the fancy vocabulary? Still trying to impress me. I knew he was trying to get my attention. Not this time, Castor. I had enough games for today. I completely ignored it.

"That's not true. I loved, past tense, Michael as my best friend. We grew up together. Moreover, he didn't fool me in any way. I was taken at gunpoint FYI. I'm not easily fooled, so please keep your stupid deductions to yourself." There was no way in hell I was letting anybody think I was a chump. *Twice.* Yeah, I have an ego. I know.

"Polly, do you have any idea what triggered him to become this way? I mean, your father was as surprised as you were when he found out what Michael was doing."

Really, Mr. FBI? Weren't you undercover? Didn't he have 'a file' as well? J. Edgar Hoover would not be proud my friend.

"Believe me, If I knew, I wouldn't be sitting in the car with you having this conversation. I just want my life back. And what did you mean by *setting shop at my house?*"

"Well, your father has agreed to cooperate with the FBI and the local police for your protection. This is the second time Michael was able to get you alone and that's unacceptable. So, Johnny has agreed to let me stay at your house for a while till this whole thing blows over at least when we catch Nabakov or Petrov."

"Johnny? What are you like BFFs, you and my dad? There's no way in hell you're staying at my place. My father has lost his marbles. Fuggedaboutit."

Yeah, you heard right.

"Polly, your father loves you very much. You have no idea

what condition he was in when you got shot. He had just been widowed and was facing the risk of losing one of his daughters. I don't think he's going to mind me dwelling in your guest room for a while."

"Are you going to be following me to work as well? I can't have you lurking around in my cemeteries."

"We have an arrangement with Mr. Roberts. Only you and him will know that there are agents at the funeral home. You are not to say a thing to anyone, even Marc or Angelo."

"I'm sorry, I can't do this. I can't lie to my colleagues. I love them too much and can't compromise their safety. I'll give in my resignation tomorrow to Uncle James."

"Polly, now's not the time to do this. On the contrary, if you resign, only then you'll be compromising their safety. We can't have anyone knowing anything." He explained.

"I didn't know that you understood Russian." I blurted.

"Oh, I do. I speak six languages. It is one of the reasons I get to do field work. Thank God, I'd have to kill myself if I had to wear one of those suits on the job."

I didn't wish to comment on his last statement. We had reached the house and my father was waiting outside. He looked disturbed. I ran to him as if I were six years old again and I had just got back from visiting the country. He held out his arms and he hugged me so hard. I shed a small tear. He pulled away from me and looked at me.

"Did that bastard hurt you?" He did a quick once over.

"No, Dad. He didn't." I smiled.

"Alright then, Anne is inside waiting for you." He kissed me on my forehead.

I ran inside the house. I couldn't find Anne anywhere. I ran up the stairs and I called for her. I could hear the TV from my bedroom. I opened the door and there was Anne sitting on my chaise longue watching a documentary about the history of corsets.

"Welcome home. You ok?"

"Yeah, I'm fine."

"So, did you send my regards to Michael?"

"Didn't have time, was getting acquainted with the gun to my head. Very bubbly personality I say. You know the usual kidnapping."

"Yeah, and hot FBI guy runs to your rescue." She stuck her tongue at me.

"Anne, seriously? I'm no damsel in distress if that's what you're implying."

"Polly, I didn't mean that. But I know you, when things get a bit heated you walk away. You've walked away from every guy who's ever wanted to get serious with you because of Michael." *Here we go with the shrinkery again.*

"What the hell are you talking about? I can't believe you're saying this to me."

"Sweetie, you don't realize this. At the back of your mind, you've always loved Michael, but you've never realized it."

"Anne, I swear to God I have never thought of Michael that way. That would be like incest, seriously. We have seen each other in diapers. Come on."

"Polly, you and Michael are no longer toddlers. Things change and people change. You've managed to sabotage every relationship you've ever been in."

"I have only been in two relationships. One lasted two years and the second lasted six months. The others didn't even qualify as dates."

"Yes, the two relationships. Your two-year relationship was in high school and he dumped you because he made you choose between him and Michael. You chose Michael. The second one, oh yeah, the pianist had opening night here in the city and yet, you told him you couldn't make it because Michael had opening night in Paris. He dumped you as well." *This shrinkery is really going to get her bitch-slapped.*

"I never got dumped, Anne. I've just only agreed to part separate ways. But if you want to consider it dumping, have it your way. I don't feel about Michael the way you think. Remember how I always used to drop everything to go see your fashion shows with mom?"

"Yeah, I know that, and I don't deny it. But you and I, it's different. We haven't changed. Michael, on the other hand, has changed a lot in so many ways that you can't see but I do."

"If he were a girl, we wouldn't be having this conversation."

"You're right, I'd be questioning your sexual orientation not that it would matter." She snorted.

"Oh, screw you!" I hit her with my pillow.

We both laughed. "By the way, what the hell are you doing in my room?"

"Don't you read the obits? My TV died."

"Why don't you use the one downstairs?"

"Too many people in the house. Besides, I'm getting a new one tomorrow."

Anne got up and turned off the TV. She told me that she was going downstairs to fix a late supper for herself. My father came up to my room with Lieutenant Prique to see if I needed anything. I was hungry but decided to retire for the evening. I closed the door, seconds later I heard a light thud on it. I opened it back again and there was Castor.

"Everything you need is in the guest bedroom." I said stiffly.

"I'm not here about my needs. I'm just here to tell you if *you need* anything, I'm just down the hall."

"I kind of figured that out. You know, here being where I live and all."

"Polly, I'm serious. If you need anything, just knock. By the way, you're not allowed to leave the house unescorted. Johnny told me about your 2 a.m. doughnut runs."

"Alright, can I please go now? I have to go to work tomorrow."

"Okay, then. Good night Polly. Beautiful nightmares."

"Good night."

I shut the door behind me. I was too tired to do anything let alone take a shower. I laid on my bed thinking about Michael and what he told me at the hotel. How he made me feel special and how he told me that he loved me- *Oh, what mendacity!* I hated it when Anne tried to analyze things. She screwed up my brains. *Ok, I was now romanticizing my kidnapping by Michael. Now, I'm officially sick and demented.* It was time to bring in the professionals. I fetched for my cellphone. Whoever invented speed dial was a genius.

"Yellow? Too busy getting kidnapped to check in?" I heard her laughing.

"Serenity, how did you know?"

"Word travels fast and I just got off the phone with Castor. He called asking me if George could drop off his book order at your house. So, naturally, that raised a lot of questions and we got to talking. We spoke for like an hour."

"Great first my dad and now with you?"

"What do you mean?"

"BFFs"

"That doesn't count, I was sort of friends with him before he ever knew you. I understand that he is living with you for the time being."

"He's not living with me. He's set up a station at our house and there are other agents outside. He's the only one who stays inside."

"Aah. Hot FBI guy protecting sexy undertaker from the Russian mob. Very cool."

"Okay, you have to lay off the erotic books."

"Not until you lay off the denial."

"It's not like that."

"Dinner tomorrow night? My treat."

Ah, deflection.

"Sure. Drinks after that? My treat."

"Yeah, why not? Get some sleep. I'll message you tomorrow where and when."

"Great. Good night. Kisses. Mwah!"

"Make sure to wear something sexy to bed in case..." I shut the phone. Note to self; tell George not to order erotic books to the shop anymore. I turned on the TV and flipped through the channels. I couldn't concentrate on what was on. My eye lids felt very heavy. I set the TV sleep timer to 15 minutes.

I began to feel somewhat cold. Damn! I must've fallen asleep again without covering myself and I was too lazy to wake up to pull the covers up. I turned around to pull the covers over my head and there he was just staring at me. His green eyes darting left and right in the dark. He came closer to me and kissed the hollow of my neck just as he did at the club. Only he didn't stop at that. I could feel his breath on my neck and ear. He kissed my shoulder all the way to my hand. He put it against his face and noticed that it was cold. He brought the cover up and brought me close to him. He caressed my hair. Thunder rumbled outside and the room lit up from the lightning. He held my face and pressed his lips against mine. They were so warm and plump. My lips parted and he caressed them with his. Then his lips started tasting different; like licking iron. He stopped and looked at me in horror. Blood started gurgling from his mouth. I screamed in horror. I noticed Michael was standing over us and he had stabbed Castor with a dagger. He came close to me and I screamed some more. My hands were full of blood. The bed started to shake. I got out of the bed to run to the door and Michael was calling after me.

"Polly, it's me!" I felt a warm hand on my cheek. I turned and it was Castor.

"Hey, you were screaming in your sleep. I'm here it's alright."

Hyperventilation and sob spasms washed over me. I was drenched. I couldn't breathe. Castor held me tight to his chest. I could hear the thunder outside. He caressed my hair. I couldn't stop crying. I didn't dare close my eyes again. "Take deep breaths, that's it... good girl. Thank God Anne and Johnny fell asleep on the couch downstairs. Are you ok? What did you see?

When I said, 'beautiful nightmares', it never occurred to me that you would listen." He let out an embarrassed chuckle.

He held my chin and stared into my eyes. "Now, Miss Polly Deuce, famous undertaker, what the hell would give you such awful night terrors?"

"Nothing. I'm fine. Sorry to wake you up." I looked down, mortified.

"You have nothing to be sorry about. Being kidnapped at gunpoint is never easy especially by someone close to you. Don't worry, I'm here to protect you and there's no way we'll let Michael, or anyone for that matter, hurt you."

"I'm fine, Castor. I can take care of myself and I thank you for your concern."

"Then how come you're still shaking?"

"Because I'm cold and someone left the window opened. If you've noticed, it's raining outside." I pointed to the window.

He got up and shut the window. I sat up straight. He was wearing grey and green plaid pajama pants with a grey t-shirt. He was buff and it was the first time I ever saw him wear cotton or short sleeves. He had a pair of legs growing out of his shoulders. I wondered how many hours he spent at the gym. I couldn't help but imagine Castor doing bench-presses with one of Angelo's tombstones with a cigarette in his mouth.

"I'm going to go downstairs to the kitchen to fetch you a glass of water." He left the room in one stride.

I was still in my work clothes. I hated falling asleep in my clothes, but I was so tired. I opened my closet and grabbed the first pair of pajamas I could lay my hands on. I went to the bathroom and locked the door behind me. I took a quick shower. I didn't feel like washing my hair. I threw on my pajamas. He had just entered the room with a sandwich along with the glass of water.

"You went to sleep without eating." He stated.

"Thank you but I'm not hungry. Please, have the sandwich." I smiled.

"I'll sit here on the chair till you fall asleep." He was walking towards the chaise longue.

"Don't you need to sleep?" I interrupted his stride.

"If you're uncomfortable, I can leave the room."

"I think you should, if you don't mind."

"Not at all." He covered me and left the room taking the sandwich with him. I got up again and opened my closet to get some thick socks from drawer. I sat on the edge of the bed and put them on. I walked back again to the side of the bed and stepped on something. I thought it was a towel or a sock. It was Castor's scarf. I must've dropped it on the floor. Haven't I just cleaned and vacuumed my room a couple of days ago? *Mmmm...* I had been meaning to return it back to him. I sniffed it and it smelled like him; musky and rosy. I folded it and put it on the chaise longue. I didn't want to risk having another night terror and him finding me spooning his scarf. *Sick, sick, sick.*

I couldn't go back to sleep. I was afraid of dreaming about Castor and Michael killing him. I got under the covers and stared out the window from my bed. I looked at the trees outside as they tangoed with the wind. It reminded me of a simpler time when Michael and I were those trees and we would tango under the rain in front of his house just for kicks. We did that so we would get sick and miss out on picture day at school. We didn't like having our pictures taken. But all that didn't matter now, it was all a lie. I was just a means to send a message, me, his mediocre friend. This slumber sobbing was giving me whiplash.

17

I woke up with a splitting headache. I hadn't gotten that much shut eye. It was seven in the morning and the trees were still tangoing. I went to the bathroom and washed my face. The two big dark swollen circles under my eyes were flashing like a dark blue neon sign for a strip joint. My eyes were hurting me. I applied a relaxant gel on my crescents. It felt cool on my skin. I brushed my teeth and noticed that the swelling went down, and the crescents were less visible. *Note to self: stop stealing Anne's skincare products and ask her where she gets them from.*

I put on a pair of black jeans and a thin turtle neck. I had a lot of digging at work today. I opened my shoe closet and saw 'his favorite Doctor Martens'. I got them out the closet and put them in a plastic bag. Went downstairs barefoot and headed for the back door and threw them in the garbage. Castor was in the kitchen having breakfast with my father. They both stared at me.

"Good morning Honey, slept well?"

"Yes, Dad thanks." I smiled faintly.

"Why did you throw out a perfect pair of boots?"

"They're not perfect and I need a new pair." I huffed.

"Honey, no need to get angry. Just asking. Tell me what color and I'll pick up a new pair for you."

"No need, Dad thanks. I have enough boots for now. I should go up and finish. I'm going to be late for work."

"Sweetie, Castor is going to drive you to work. He's responsible for you now. You can't go anywhere unescorted. We've notified Uncle James and you are not to say anything to anybody about undercover agents at the parlor."

"I understand. May I go now?"

"You didn't even say 'Good Morning' to Castor."

"I will when my babysitter takes me to work." I smiled at them. Castor tittered and sipped his coffee making believe he was reading the paper.

I ran back upstairs and put on my steel toed work boots. I piled my hair into one lump on my head. I needed a haircut. I got my backpack and packed some evening clothes since I was going out with Serenity tonight. I didn't want to have to come back home and change. I threw in my make-up kit and my knee-high five-inch heel leather boots. I went back to the bathroom and slapped on some concealer and tons of black eyeliner. I went back downstairs, and my dad handed me a paper bag. *Yes, my dad packs my breakfast or lunch from time to time as if I were still in elementary school. Get over it.* I gave him a peck on the cheek. He told me that Anne had already left at 6:30 to beat the traffic. I'll try and give her a call during the day. Castor was warming up my car.

I opened the car door and got inside without a word. "Why, Good Morning to you too, Miss Deuce! This is your Captain Castor Black for..." I cut him off.

"Umm...I'm not a morning person so please stop it. I just want to get to work."

"Yes, Boss." He army saluted me with his hand.

"Stop that. Not funny." I kept a stiff upper lip.

"But you are my boss. I'm not being funny. Mr. Roberts agreed to give me a job at the parlor. I'll be working with this guy, Elijah. Another agent will be assigned there. If anyone asks, I'm your mom's little cousin who came back to live with you guys. My parents died when I was 4 and I'm staying with my Uncle Johnny till I can get my act together."

"Oh my God!!!!!!!!!!!!AAAAAAAAAAAAAAAAAAAHHHHH-HHHHHHHHHHHHHHHHHHHHHHHHHHHHHHHHH-HHH!!!!!!!!!!!!!!!!!!!!!!!!!! Are you nuts? Everyone knows that you are Sandy's brother. Are you trying to drive me mad?!"

"Actually, your colleagues don't even know anything

about Sandy, and you were the only one to see me at your mom's funeral. Serenity knows me from her book shop, but I gave her a head's up. Other than that, only your dad's friends, who are my colleagues know me as Sandy's brother. I am seldom with Sandy at the catering business."

"Why, oh why did you tell me now?"

"Protocol. Besides, I didn't want to upset you."

"And saying it now makes it better?" I swear my eyeballs were going to pop out of their sockets.

"Listen, I have to remain at your side at all times for now. Something may go down. Especially in your line of work, many things can go wrong and I'm not going to risk it. I can't explain everything to you. All in due time."

"I don't like this. Uncle James just made me assistant supervisor at work and that's a big shitload. I can't have you making mistakes. Not to sound too pedantic but what the hell do you know about this business?"

"I'm a fast learner. I don't mind you bossing me around." He winked at me. We stopped a few blocks away from the funeral home.

"What now?" I sighed.

"Give me a minute."

He opened my glove compartment and got out a little transparent box. He opened it and the contents appeared to be contact lenses. He put them on. The once beautiful green eyes were now dark chocolate brown. He took out another box. It looked like a jewelry box and removed from it what seemed to be a wedding band. He put the gold band on his left ring finger. He turned to me. "So, how do I look?"

I haven't the chance to look at Castor that morning. But it seems the moron dyed his beautiful reddish hair black. His eyebrows were a bit darker. He did look like a whole different person. He did look like someone from my mother's side of the family. They all had that dark shiny black hair. My mom's Aunt lives in London and is married to an art director. She never had children. The last time I saw Aunt Chloe was at mom's funeral.

Castor started the car again and drove us to work. As we pulled in, I saw Marc standing outside.

"Good morning, Hon. Listen, Angelo told me that Mr. Roberts is bringing in another undertaker to work with Elijah. He didn't say who. Thank God, because we could use another hand. By the way, congrats Ms. Assistant Supervisor." He nudged me playfully.

"Thank you, Sweetie. I couldn't have done it without any of you." I nudged him back.

Marc looked over my shoulder and asked: "Are we dating and not sharing with Marc?" I hated it when he referred to himself in the third person.

"Eww. Of course, not." I turned around and Castor was walking towards us. "That's the new undertaker Mr. Roberts was talking about. He happens to be my mom's little cousin."

He whispered in my ear. "I'm sure there's nothing little about him."

I elbowed Marc. He was such a gossip bitch.

"Hi, my name's Charles Manson. I'm Polly's second cousin and I'm the new undertaker." He shook hands with Marc.

"Your name's Charles Manson. Are you for real dude? How? Why?"

"Well, Polly's maternal grandfather's name is Charles and my mother married someone with the last name Manson. Get my drift?" Castor kept a straight face. *Fuck my life. I was going to burst in tears of laughter.*

"Oooookay." Marc smiled. We all walked inside, and Marc marched to his workplace. I could see him smiling from the back of his head.

Uncle James was at the front desk. He came up to greet us. He gave me a big hug and shook hands with Castor. Uncle James spoke in a low tone.

"Charles, have Polly show you around. She's the best and you'll have Elijah with you to pick up some of the slack. The other agent should be arriving at lunch time I'm told. If you do anything to compromise the safety of Polly, I will exsanguinate you and use your blood as paint for my office. Other than that, welcome to the family." Uncle James grinned at him. I have never seen that side of him before. Come to think of it, I have never seen any other side to Uncle James. Hell, I have never seen the psychopath side of Michael either.

Castor and I walked outside to the cemetery. I was looking for Angelo and Elijah. No sign of either of them. We walked around to the other side.

"Why was Uncle James talking to you that way? I thought he liked you."

"He does." He chuckled.

"You lost me."

"Polly, this morning your father threatened to rip my guts out and use my intestines as a jump rope. John and James love me, but they love you more and hey, they need time to get over the fact that I almost killed you. Needless to say, we get along but believe me, you have no idea how bad it was when you were in a coma. Doctors thought you weren't going to make it. There was this loudmouth doctor, he had advised your dad and Mr. Roberts to make funeral arrangements because he was sure that you weren't going to make it. So, they almost used him as a punching bag...they shoved him against a wall and were brought in for questioning. Vincent, Eddie, Francis and my supervisor pulled a few strings. You know FBI trumps police, so we got them out the same day. Enter Doctor York."

"You're kidding me, right? I have never seen my father lay a hand with the intention on hurting somebody in my life. Neither have I seen Uncle James do such a thing as well." The Book of Revelations keeps on giving.

"It's true. But we left out all those unpleasant details. That doctor was an ass anyway. He deserved it. I mean, here you are, all better, clobbering FBI agents, getting kidnapped and digging graves." He nudged me and smiled.

"Polly! Is that you over there!?" I heard someone shout.

"Angelo! Is that you!?" I shouted back.

"Yeah, can you please come and give me a hand?"

"On my way!" Castor and I paced quickly towards Angelo.

I saw Angelo putting the final touches on a tombstone and Elijah assembling big pieces of marble. I stiffened.

"Hey, you must be the new guy, Charles Manson, right?"

"Yes, nice to meet you. Aren't you Angelo?" Castor shaking hands with Angelo.

"That's true. And this is Elijah. You'll be working with him under Polly's supervision." Angelo pointing to Elijah.

As Angelo explained to Castor certain points of his job description, I watched Elijah use the rest of the mineral adhesive on the marble. I just couldn't move. I never did like preparing that type of burial chamber. We were standing in front of the mausoleum of the richest families in the area. And that burial chamber was not going to go inside of it. It was to be placed near it. That's how we buried babies here. That's probably the hardest part of my job. Burying a baby who can't even speak and barely walk.

"Am I doing something wrong Polly? You seem dissatisfied with my work." Elijah pointed out.

"No, you're doing a great job. I'm just observing. Make sure you use the metal planks to press the marble correctly on the sides. Those parallelogram-looking cradles can be quite tricky." I stayed for half an hour to help Elijah with the metal planks.

I turned to Castor and Angelo who were engaged in work-related conversation. "I'm going inside to see Marc. If you boys need anything, you'll know where to find me."

I walked as fast as I could back inside the parlor and headed for Marc's work station. He looked busy and he surely could've used a hand.

"Polly, I'm so glad you're here. Sarah went out to run errands for me."

"Why don't you ask Elijah? You two get along, don't you?"

"Yes, we do. He keeps asking me about you. I keep telling him you're off-limits. It's like talking to a wall. So, now I'm avoiding him. The guy can't take a hint. He's pissing me off."

"I'll have a talk with Uncle James although he hasn't said anything to me or made any advances towards me."

"No, you don't. I'm going to talk to Mr. James. He is beginning to annoy *me*." He insisted.

"Alright, have it your way. So, where's the baby?"

"Over there. She's ready." He pointed at the slab in the corner of the room. It was covered.

"How did she die?"

"SIDs."

"What?"

"Sudden Infant Death. Those rich people stuff their babies' cribs with too much frilly crap. She was barely three months old. Her mother found her dead yesterday afternoon."

A bit judgmental, aren't we? But Marc was being Marc. Always over emotional when he has any child on his slab.

"You mean she just suffocated from too many things in her crib?"

"Yes. You always must keep an infant on her side at that age. Not on her stomach neither on her back in case she spits up."

"I thought that SIDs has nothing to do with that and that babies should sleep on their backs. I helped Elijah work on the crib burial chamber. It was coming together quite nicely. I assume the funeral is tomorrow because there's no way we can fill that thing with moist dirt."

"The funeral is at five. By the way, it's Angelo's birthday tomorrow. I'll take care of the present. We'll meet at Club Thingy at eight."

"Marc, no one will make it on time. You're the only one who doesn't do any digging around here. How about we make it at nine?"

"Yeah, sure no problem. It's a surprise party anyway."

"Surprise party? He hates surprises."

"Yeah, I'm getting back at him for throwing me one." He smiled.

"What did you dress the baby?"

"Christening gown."

"Why?"

"She was supposed to be baptized this week. You know the rest."

"Spunkie." I muttered.

"What is that?"

"Spunkie is the lost soul of a child who hasn't been baptized."

"That's morbid, Polly." It was so funny when Marc's eyes popped.

"It's a fact." I blurted. Well, it was a Catholic fact. *I think. Maybe something did register from Sunday school.*

Sarah had just entered the room. She was a very sweet person, a bit chatty but she never gossiped. She always tries to invite me for a cup of coffee, and I keep turning her down. I made a point of inviting her to Angelo's party. Marc decided he didn't need my help since Sarah had come back early. He insisted on showing me the baby. *Ah, Morbid Marc.*

He unveiled the baby. It was hard to believe she was dead. She looked like she was sleeping. Her little fingers were rigid, and her hands looked like she was reaching out to me. She had light brown hair. He thin lips puckered as if she were still suckling on a teat. I could see that Sarah had painted her lips a rosy pink and put a bit on her cheeks as well. I just wanted to hold that baby and cradle her. She'll never get to celebrate her first birthday. She'll never get to have her first kiss or fall in love or get her heart-broken. I think God didn't want to subject her to such pain. It was better that way.

"I have to go now. Have to see if Elijah and the new guy are getting along."

"Sure thing. Go, I'll catch up with you later."

"Alright. Bye Marc."

"Bye, Sarah."

"Bye Polly." She waved with her surgical glove.

I went back outside to see how Castor was getting along

with the others. The newbies were working on a new mausoleum across the cemetery. I knew Angelo was going to need me there later. I went up to the crib burial chamber and heard Castor giving Elijah a crash course in what seemed to be about coffin texts.

"Coffin texts were the magical symbols and spells written by Egyptians on the coffins of the deceased. Their only function was to guarantee that the soul survived the afterlife."

"That's interesting so can you tell me about the use of tombstones?" Elijah asked.

"Tombstones or headstones dated back to the Stone Age when..."

"Alright, you two, back to work." I clapped my hands together.

"Charles, you should be working and not giving the employees here a crash course in symbolism." I said loudly.

"I'm sorry, Polly. We are working and almost done. It's just that Elijah and I share a lot of common interests, that's all." *Jerk-off is going to have a lot of common interests with my foot if he keeps this up.*

"Okay, great then. You and he can get a room later. Back to work."

Elijah wasn't very pleased with my demeanor. I didn't care. He was asking inappropriate questions about me to Marc and I wasn't going to have him get all chummy with Castor. It was already too complicated having Mr. FBI living at my house, let alone working with me. I couldn't talk to anybody about my problems. I was going to see Serenity today for dinner, but I needed to talk to Uncle James. I needed to fix this situation before it became a problem. I loved my job too much. He was also harassing Marc. This was getting ridiculous.

I was scheduled to lead orientation for the newbies at eleven. I went to Uncle James' office to get the hand-outs and talk to him. He was on the phone and motioned for me to stay. I went to the espresso machine and pulled two single espressos. He was already done.

"Polly, thanks for the espresso. I really needed it. Are you ready for orientation?"

"Yes, I am. I'm just picking up the hand-outs and taking them to my work station."

"Ok. Finish your coffee and go. Come on, have a seat with me. We barely talk anymore."

"Uncle James all we do is talk. You're at my house almost every day." I smiled.

"You don't look very happy. Is Castor making you uncomfortable at work? I can have him transferred to one of the other cemeteries nearby."

"Actually, it's not Castor. It's Elijah. He's become too chummy with Castor in less than a day and I don't like it."

"But that's a good thing, isn't it?" He gave me a perplexed look.

"Oh, yeah don't get me wrong. It is a good thing but ... you know something it's nothing. It's not my place. I have to get back to work." I got up and took my hand-outs.

"Stop! Turn! Walk back here, young lady." Uncle James was smiling ironically.

"What's wrong? I promise I won't let anyone know anything. I won't even tell Clarissa and Kathy." He said in a feminine voice.

"Who's Clarissa and Kathy?" I was confused.

"My imaginary gossip bitches." He did do a good woman's voice.

"Elijah keeps asking Marc if I'm available. Marc keeps telling him that I'm not and that I'm off-limits. Marc is planning on telling you himself, but I beat him to the punch. Marc is really annoyed with this and now Elijah is all chummy with Castor because, and I'm sure, he thinks he's really related to me and that he can get to me in some way."

"I understand. Is he a good employee?"

"Oh, other than that he is a very good employee. He always follows my orders. I actually enjoy working with him." I didn't want him to lose his job. I just wanted him to lay off my business.

"I'll talk to him. I'll tell him the story of how I tried to castrate my cat when I was sixteen. Poor Sherlock." He sighed. Uncle James has an imaginary cat for his psycho story-telling purposes.

"I have to get back to work." Ignoring Uncle James' last statement.

Orientation went well. Castor and Elijah were sitting front row. Sophia, from Purchasing, had drawn out a chart of how to order supplies. She was very anal when it came to these things. I didn't blame her. As a former accountant, I used to sometimes get five purchase orders for the same order number and hell would break loose.

After explaining all the guidelines to the newbies and answering a series of questions, it was time for lunch. Elijah was ogling me. I wanted to sucker punch him. I tried not to look at Castor all day and this was becoming very tiresome. I was digging his new look. I avoided him during lunch break like the plague.

At around 5, I received a message from Serenity.

Meet me De Niro's 6 :30? I'm in the mood for Italiano.

That's good I brought some nice clothes with me in my backpack. I had the feeling she was going to invite me to De Niro's. I messaged her back.

Gr8. Can't w8 2 c u.xoxo.

I was so happy. Then it hit me, Castor wasn't going to let me out of his sight. That was the reason in the first place he got a job here, so that he could protect me. *PFFFFFT!* Maybe, I should give him something to do and leave without him knowing. I can open his locker and get the keys to my car.

I went outside and told him and Elijah that I needed to show them a blueprint of the mausoleum being built across the cemetery. Uncle James never fully relied on contractors to build mausoleums for him that's why he had Angelo. He always oversaw the process. They were already prepping for tomorrow's funeral and promised to go help Angelo. That should keep them both busy till six. I went back inside and went to the bathroom. Uncle James had installed two showers in the ladies' bathroom. He had done this because I was the only female undertaker and there was Sarah who worked overtime with Marc. Sarah and I sometimes had to conduct services. So, Uncle James installed showers so we wouldn't have to go home and prep. We had to have a way to wash off the smell of embalming fluid and soil.

I took a quick shower and got dressed. It had been a while since I wore platform heels due to my accident. I slapped on some makeup and went out looking for the superintendent. He had all the keys. He opened Castor's locker and took the keys to my car. I punched out and ran towards my Volvo.

I put the key in the ignition, and it wouldn't turn. I tried again. I saw Castor coming out of the parlor. *Oh, crap!* He walked towards the car and tapped on the window.

"And where are we going?" He was grinning. *Jerk-off.*

"'We' (*I motioned with my index finger between me and him)* are not going anywhere. What did you do to my car key?"

"Since you asked so kindly. I knew that you would pull such a stunt so I put a dummy key in my locker because I knew the superintendent would open the locker for you." He was smiling crookedly now.

"Castor, I'm not taking you with me to meet up with Serenity. This is ridiculous. I can't have you lurking around all the time. I have a life you know." *Frustration level 7.*

"Oh, I know. Don't fret. I know you're meeting her at De Niro's at six-thirty."

He went to the other side and opened the passenger seat and got in. "How did you know?"

"How did I know?" He asked himself out loud, sarcastically. "I'm FBI Baby. You're under my surveillance 24/7. The only way you're going to get rid of me is to kill me."

"I bet there's already a hit on you. Problem solved." I rolled my eyes at him.

"Listen, I'll drop you at De Niro's. There are two agents over there. Don't worry, they won't be listening in on your conversation with Serenity. I wouldn't do that to her- and you."

"But we're going for drinks after that."

"I know. I've got everything arranged. Don't worry. You won't be seeing any more of me for today."

I drove to De Niro's and Castor was quiet the whole time. So not like him. When we reached the restaurant, he got out and opened the door for me before I could switch off the ignition.

"Take care, bye." He smiled.

"Bye." I told him.

He drove off with my car and I went inside the restaurant. Serenity had already ordered red wine and appetizers for the both of us. She got up and gave me a big hug.

"So, how are you?"

"I'm fine but I don't think that I need to update you on anything that much since you and Castor talk a lot." *Yeah, I was being petty and bitter.*

"Oh, no Sweetie. It's just because I'm your best friend he feels that I should know what's going on as well. But you seem miffed about all this."

"I am. I didn't know about any plan till this morning. He's staying at my house, across from my bedroom. He wakes up in the middle of the night if I have night terrors. He's just always there and I can't breathe. Now, he's working with me. I'm going to suffocate."

"Night terrors? The only time you started getting those is six months after you started your job at the parlor. Are they coming back?"

"No, not those night terrors."

"Then, what? Did Michael do something to you? You can tell me, I won't tell anyone." She seemed very concerned. It dawned upon me what she was insinuating.

"Oh, no Honey. Nothing even close to that. It's just bad dreams."

"Polly, there are bad dreams and there are night terrors."

"Serenity, seriously there's nothing. I think it's just a one-night thing you know from all the stress. I'd rather not talk about it. Do you mind?" *I need to learn to keep my damn mouth shut. I keep forgetting that everyone around me has minored in shrinkery.*

"I don't at all. But you'll have to tell me soon. I'm not going to push my luck now."

"Thanks. By the way, what has Castor been telling you?"

"Only the things I need to know in order not to blow his cover. But *you* haven't told me anything yet."

I sat there for like one hour telling Serenity how Michael kidnapped me and how he had a gun to my head. I told her how he said that he loved me, and I also told her what he'd said in the video he sent with me to the FBI. After a two-course meal, Serenity's eyes popped out as if she saw a ghost.

18

"Serenity, are you ok?"

"Oh, my goodness, Polly! You love Michael!!!!"

"What the fuck?! I thought you were choking to death or saw a ghost!" *Here we go again with the shrinkery. I did an internal eyeroll.*

"Same effect. I reached an epiphany!"

"You're out of your mind! I don't love him and even if there was the slightest residue of emotion for him it's all gone now." I think she needed to get her head checked.

"Then why were you so disappointed?" she frowned.

"I was hurt not disappointed, hurt." Emphasizing on the last word.

"Same thing. Yams, sweet potatoes." She threw her hands in the air.

"No, it's not. If I were disappointed like you said I am, that would be that I expected something only to be let down. That is surely not the case. I am hurt because he played with my feelings, being since he knows me well, in order to play some sick twisted game with the FBI. He had no concern for my well-being. He just used me." I was staring at my plate of untouched ravioli. I then began to tell her about what Anne had told me. *Ok, I may need to get my head checked.*

"I still say I'm right. Even Anne sees it. You just haven't realized it. I think you're both; hurt and disappointed. Why don't you just get over him?"

"Get over what? I never dated him."

"Well, you may have well done that. Your relationship shares the same characteristics as a romantic one minus the denial and romance." *Shrinkery fuckin 2.0. Don't they usually wait a year before an update to an app?*

"That's cruel. I'm in no mood for this."

She got up and brought her chair next to mine. She laid my head on her shoulder and held me. She softly said: "I'm sorry but it is what it is. He's loved you for a very long time and you have loved him as well, unconsciously at least. Ummm...let's get out of here and go to Piper's Pub. We need hard liquor and music."

Oh, I needed hard liquor alright. Everyone around me was psycho-analyzing my relationship with Michael. Whoever said that psychology was a pseudo-science was right. I saw no merit to all this babble. You cannot grow up with someone the way I did and not have some connection. There was love no doubt about it, but it was in no way of a sexual nature. Considering my last encounter with Michael, I am having second thoughts about his part. Be as it may, we have always had a special friendship. Never once has he or I, ever crossed or felt a need to cross this boundary.

She ordered the check and we were out the door in minutes. I couldn't tell where the agents were. I didn't care. I just kept thinking about Michael and how he hurt me. I was a complete mess. We reached Piper's Pub at around nine. I hadn't been there in quite a while. I remember the bartender having a thing for Serenity. We'd always have way too many drinks on the house. We entered the pub, and everyone was greeting Serenity. I headed straight for the bar. Serenity followed me. We sat down on the high stools.

"Thank God they finally changed them." She grinned.

I immediately knew what she was talking about. "It's about time. The old bar stools were giving my quads a good work-out"

"I'm having tequila shots, you?"

"Make that a double order."

"Ooh, I like Tequila Polly, she's much more fun that Martini Polly."

"I can't be your designated driver tonight. How are we going to go home?" I reminded her.

"Babe, we'll call a cab and George can pick up my car tomorrow morning. Drink and don't worry."

"No worries." I downed the first shot.

The shots kept coming in. I think I had about eight. I began to feel a bit queasy, then I realized I hadn't really eaten anything today. I barely had touched my food at De Niro's, I had maybe five or six morsels; other than that, *nothing.* I was too busy avoiding Castor that I forgot to eat lunch at work. I was proud that one of us was holding down her liquor. *Go Serenity!* I made my way to the bathroom. I wasn't even drunk, very aware of my surroundings, but my knees gave. I stood up again and rushed to the bathroom. I locked the stall door and hugged the porcelain throne. I let out the sweetest heave. All at once without gagging once. I felt lightheaded. I looked at my watch. It was only ten o'clock. My goodness, I had managed to down eight shots of tequila in forty-five minutes. Wow, I was in denial. Oh well, I gave my liver a pretty good workout. I was feeling very woozy. I decided to take a five-minute nap sitting on floor near the porcelain throne. I heard someone knock on the stall. My body refused to move.

"Polly, are you alright? Open the door!"

Serenity really shouldn't drink so much. Her voice sounded so hoarse and manly. The door kept pounding but I couldn't move. Someone kicked the door in, but I barely could see who it was. I just wanted to sleep.

I woke up around one in the morning with a stabbing headache. My mouth was dry, and my head was spinning. No more alcohol for me. I looked around and I wasn't in my room. I knew this house. Oh my God! I must've passed out and Serenity brought me to her place by cab. I was wearing pajamas. She must've undressed me. Poor thing. I marched to the kitchen and the lights were on. I could smell the coffee from her percolator.

I heard company. *Who?* She lived by herself and would never let anyone in at such an hour. I reached the kitchen and there I saw two mugs and Castor at her kitchen table.

"Polly, how are you feeling? You scared me to death. You were away in the bathroom for half an hour and you wouldn't open the door. I thought something had happened to you or someone did something to you. This is my fault! I'm so sorry." I wasn't used Serenity being apologetic.

"Baby, I had eight shots in less than an hour and I hadn't really eaten anything today. It's not your fault. I fucked up your evening."

"I shouldn't have pushed you about the other matter then..." I cut her off. Please, Serenity. It's one in the morning. I don't care and you're my best friend and you're just looking out for me. Just get me an Aspirin and cup of coffee, we'll call it even. She dashed out the kitchen to fetch me an Aspirin.

Castor was pouring me a cup of coffee.

"I understand being here, the dizziness, the queasiness and all the stupidity I did tonight. Where do you fit in this picture?" I demanded.

"When Serenity realized you had been gone for a long time, she followed you to the bathroom. You were unresponsive and when she went out to get the bartender to give her the keys to the stall, one of the agents called me to come. I was nearby. It took me two minutes to get there. One of the agents, appearing to be a client at the pub, broke the door down. You were barely conscious."

"So, you carried me out the pub in front of everyone. My God, I must've embarrassed Serenity. Everyone knows her there."

"Actually no, the bartender lead us through the back door to where they take out the trash. I carried you and I covered you from top to toe with my trench. No one saw you, don't worry. But you scared me to be honest. Were you trying to commit suicide or something? Eight shots in forty-five minutes? Food or no food, that's too much alcohol in such a short time-frame. Were you trying to kill yourself?" He glared at me.

"Maybe I was. It's none of your Goddamn business to question me. I'm not a criminal you take to your headquarters for questioning. If I want to drink myself blind, I'll do that. Next time please don't come if I'm unconscious. Stay out of my business." I glared back at him.

Serenity interrupted me with a bottle of Aspirin. "I'm going to sleep. I have to wake up in a couple of hours, receiving an order at seven. If you want to go home, your clothes are in the guest's bathroom. If not, you know where everything is here. Stay as long as you like. I already told your father that you were spending the night here."

"Alright. Good night."

Serenity marched to her room. I felt bad for making her feel bad. I turned to Castor; "I think you should go home now. I'm staying here."

"I'm sorry, I can't. Strict orders. It's protocol."

"I can't have you stay here. Serenity didn't say anything about you which means it's your cue to leave. You have the keys to my house so please go."

He puckered his lips. "Nope, I have to stay here. Whether you like it or not and Serenity didn't say anything because I had already told her that I'll be crashing on her couch. I just can't leave you here like a chump."

"Fine have it your way." I took two Aspirins and didn't bother drinking the coffee. My head was still spinning. I marched to my room and locked the door behind me. I didn't want him coming in my room at night.

I woke up at seven in the morning with the world's biggest hangover. I'm never drinking alcohol again – till nine tonight, then all bets are off. I went to the kitchen and had three glasses of cold water. I searched for the Aspirin but couldn't find it. I saw a letter on the kitchen table addressed to me.

Dear Polly,

I hope you're feeling better. Castor left you some pills for hangovers near the fruit bowl on the counter. DON'T TAKE ANY ASPIRIN WITH IT! Be nice! Take care and love you.

-Serenity-

I went straight for the fruit bowl and read the instructions. TAKE TWO PILLS EVERY FOUR HOURS. I took two pills and gulped down another glass of water. I realized that Castor wasn't on the couch and the quilt cover had been folded.

Great! He must've gone to his house. How the heck was I supposed to get to work? And there was no chance in hell I was going to work in my platform heels. Oh God, why have you forsaken me? Why must FBI hunk make my life miserable and carry me around like a keg of beer from a bar? *Wow, my hangover is starting to wear off.* Mr. FBI really knows how to cure a hangover. Holding on to that last thought, I heard the front door open. It was Castor. He was holding my backpack. I wonder what it was doing with him. He looked too serious for 7:20 in the morning. He handed me my backpack.

"I'll meet you out front in your car in thirty minutes. You'll find in your bag a fresh change of clothes. Anne packed for you. Did you have breakfast?"

"No, I just woke up and took two of those hangover pills. I can already feel their effect. Thank you."

"Yeah, good.... you're welcome." He pursed his lips together. He didn't look at me the whole time. That was so unlike him. He's usually in my face. Maybe he was beginning to follow his exact job description. I must say that I was thankful for him getting my clothes.

I went upstairs and took a quick hot shower. Thank you, Serenity, for the great smelling shower gel. I wreaked of alcohol. This was so unlike me. I couldn't imagine what I had put her through last night. I was still feeling a bit weak. I got out of the shower and went into the bedroom. I opened the backpack. I'm so going to kill Anne when I see her. She had packed the tightest pair of jeans she could find in my closet. I mean, the cellulite on my thighs were going to breed more cellulite just by wearing those jeans. Thank God for overalls at work. At least she packed a t-shirt, a short sleeve tight one. Great, my love handles will get an awesome tan at twenty two degrees Fahrenheit and no sun.

No bra? She happened to pack underwear but no bra. Okay, I'm digging her a plot today. How was I supposed to go to work now? I let my hair down over my chest. I wore my trench and headed for the door. My car was idled. Castor was inside and I could hear the music blasting from my stereo. I opened the door and got in the car. He didn't flinch. He was listening to a metal song which I couldn't recognize. I didn't even want to ask him. I reached work on time. I ran to the locker room and got into my overalls, luckily, I found my sports bra in my cubby. I went to the front desk to pick up my roster and suddenly Elijah appeared in front of me.

"Good morning Polly. Sarah told me to tell you that Uncle James will be conducting the five o'clock service. He'll meet us up at Club Thingy for Angelo's surprise party." He spoke in a low tone.

"Okay, great then. Have Charles start helping you assemble the pedestal for The Cochrane's mausoleum. I'll meet you there in fifteen, okay?"

"Yeah, sure. I didn't see Charles yet? Didn't he carpool with you?"

"Yes, I'm sure he's back somewhere. He knows to how read the roster and I'm sure he'll be there at the mausoleum. Is everything prepared for the five o'clock funeral?"

"Yes, it just needs your final touch." He smiled

"Thank you, Elijah. Meet you out." I gave him a one thumb up. What was that about? I needed to talk to Marc. I went to his work station and found Castor there. He was handing Marc a fifty-dollar bill.

"Thanks for reserving the tables at the club. You're my man, Charles! I'm glad you liked Angelo's present. See you tonight."

"Don't mention it. See you tonight." Castor was grinning. He hadn't noticed my presence. I was surprised not to see Marc working on a dead body. He was arranging some supplies.

"Marc, please don't tell me you bought something lavish for Angelo? I mean fifty bucks each of us? What on earth did you buy him? A diamond shovel? We're going to be like twenty people tonight at his party. That's a grand!"

Marc turned to me and lowered his glasses. "First, it's twenty-five bucks each and that would sum up to five hundred dollars. Second, I got him cufflinks with his initials engraved on them. Third, it's Charles who offered to pay for your share."

"Yeah, I think I forgot my wallet at home. But you should've asked me first." I frowned.

"Oh, unwind your lace panties why don't you? He's your mother's cousin. Your second cousin. He's family. Get a grip, it's just twenty-five bucks. I've known you to have pride but you're just being a stick in the mud."

"Not funny. You know, I wanted to talk to you about something but now I changed my mind." I just wanted to slap him. Marc has never spoken to me in such a manner. I wasn't in the mood today for explaining myself. I marched out of the room.

"But, Polly! Hey, I didn't mean it that way! Please come back!" I just slammed the door and he was still calling me. I marched straight to The Cochrane mausoleum. Angelo was working with a router cutting out a cross made from black marble. Elijah and two workers were on scaffolds. The Cochrane mausoleum was one of the biggest and tallest mausoleums in the graveyard. Castor had his black hair in a French braid. *Funny.* I didn't have the time to look at him last night or this morning. I began to wonder who was the second agent that was supposed to arrive yesterday. If I had to ask, that would mean having to talk to Castor and he was giving me the silent treatment. Why was he being such a jerk? He knows that he's been crossing some lines with me. I'm the one who should be giving him the silent treatment. He was building the pedestal by himself. Interesting.

Now I know how legs tend to grow out of shoulders. Angelo motioned to me. He needed help. I was the only person, besides Angelo, who knew how to work a router with precision. I had years of practice with my Dad. While Anne sewed dresses with my mom, Dad had taught me how to use a router for various materials; from wood to granite. I put on my gloves and goggles and got to work. He stopped the router.

"What's wrong? Come on you're not going to do this alone." I huffed.

"Oh, no it's not that. I need your expertise O Wise One." It was funny seeing Angelo bow his head to me. *Please don't tell me you weren't using the diamond tip router bit.*

"Shoot."

"I'm about to cut out of this black marble a Celtic cross. But the Cochranes don't want the arms of the cross protruding beyond the circle. Why would they want that?"

"That would be the Sun Cross, where the whole symbol is encompassed in a circle. This cross appeared in the Bronze Age, yet the Catholic church adopted it and incorporated the Latin Cross in it. Early versions of it in Ireland don't show the arms protruding. So, I don't think you have anything to worry about."

"Uhuh. Interesting. Want to cut?"

"Sure do."

Angelo held the marble as I made an early version of the Celtic cross, hence Sun Cross. The striations were becoming jagged, so I had to change the bit. I didn't, not once, lift up my head to look at Castor. I was proud of myself and pleased with my work. It had taken me and Angelo about 3 hours to cut, buff, polish and erect the cross. I was full of marble dust. I had to go prep for the five o'clock funeral. I didn't feel like dealing with Marc or his bitch alter ego.

I went to the service room and the florists were decorating the room with Baby's Breath and some other type of flower I couldn't identify. *Go figure.* I saw Marc crossing the hall with the small white coffin. I went to the bathroom and changed into another overall. I opened my bag and got out some money. I went to Castor's cubby and I slipped him the twenty-five bucks. I made my way down the hall, to Marc's. He was putting the baby girl in the coffin. It was only three. Marc looked up at me.

"Her mother is coming in. She wants some alone time with her."

"Ok. I have to fill the cradle chamber with some dirt."

"Polly?"

"Yes?"

"Is everything ok with you? You seem agitated."

"Everything's good. No need to worry." I half-smiled.

"You said that you wanted to talk to me about something."

"I thought I did but now I don't. Problem solved."

"Okay. I'll see you tonight then?"

"Yes. Of course. By the way, Elijah won't be bothering you anymore with questions about me."

"He hasn't so far today." He winked at me.

I went back out to the cemetery and filled the cradle with about twenty inches of dirt. When it was time to bury that beautiful baby girl, I had to pour some more dirt on the coffin till it was full to the rim. Her mother never stopped sobbing for a moment. Castor looked staggered. I couldn't call the cradle what it was; a crypt. Castor and I shut the crypt by placing a very heavy thick marble slab over it. The mourners had to drag the mother away. She lost it when I started using silicone to glue the slab. I felt like I was burying somebody alive because that baby didn't look dead to me, or so I had wished. A mother shouldn't have to bury her child and a child shouldn't have to bury her mother- so soon.

Castor was waiting for me outside in my Volvo. He was still ignoring me. When we reached home, I found my father and Anne in the kitchen. Lieutenant Prique was tearing some salad leaves. My father gave me the biggest hug and my sister gave me the biggest grin. "I'm going to kill you." I mouthed to her.
"Hey kid, how's that hangover?"

I stared bluntly at my father. Who told him? It must've

been Castor. I'm going to rip out his beautiful white skin and use it as wallpaper.

"Good."

"Polly, what did you eat today?"

"I don't remember."

"She ate nothing, Johnny. She had a cup of green tea for lunch." Castor answered my father as if he were a teacher's pet. *Bastard.* I'm going to make him my bitch if he keeps this up.

"Oh really?" My father raised an eyebrow.

"Dad, I had a really bad night. I drank too many shots *too fast*. I'm fine now. Please tell Agent Asshole to stop telling on me as if he were my bratty little brother." I pointed to Castor.

My father and Lieutenant Prique cracked up laughing. Anne, however, made kissing faces behind Castor's back. Everyone was a comedian today. I had peas and carrots for supper and went upstairs. I locked my bedroom door and headed for the shower. I put my blow dryer on full blast and wore a long velvet midnight blue dress, not to forget the platform heels. I saw that Castor's scarf was still on my chaise longue. I applied the final touches to my makeup and headed for the guest room. I knocked on the door and he opened it. He looked surprised.

"This is your scarf. We have to leave in a while and if you ever cross me again, I'll skin you and use your skin as wallpaper." I threatened.

"You'd love that, wouldn't you?" He smiled.

I handed him the scarf and just marched right back to my bedroom without even looking back at him once. I called Serenity. She was wiped out. I tried getting her to come to Angelo's party, but she said she was too tired and just wanted to go home. I went downstairs and Anne was all dressed up. "Going somewhere?" I asked.

"Yeah, Marc invited me to Angelo's birthday. Now I get to look at you and Castor." She giggled.

"Anne, you can't say stuff like that. Marc thinks he's mom's cousin!"

"I know that but I'll be the only one who knows what's

going on. It's just so exciting."

"Okay, you need to go out more. Get some vitamin D and fresh air."

She stuck her tongue at me. Very mature. I heard someone honking outside. "That's my cue. Marc's waiting outside. See you." *Ugh!!!!!!*

I went into the kitchen and my father was still with Lieutenant Prique. They were going out to meet up with the rest of the gang at Vincent's place. My father kissed me goodbye. I stayed in the kitchen and had a cup of coffee. I looked at the clock and it was almost nine. I went upstairs and Castor's door was still closed. I knocked and no answer. I opened the door just a little and no one was inside. I closed the door and headed downstairs. I looked out the driveway and he was standing in front of my car smoking a cigarette. I didn't see him leave the house. I put on my coat and grabbed my purse. He got into the car and I followed. There was quite a bit traffic on our way. As we moved forward, we saw the cause of the traffic. It was the result of a hit and run. The victim survived. Thank God.

"How do you do it?" He suddenly asked.

"Do what?"

"Bury babies and go to a party in the evening." He stated.

"I'm an undertaker. I lay people to rest. It's what I do. Don't you kill people and go to barbecues?"

"Not in that order. But it's different. I pursue bad people. I rarely run across a dead infant."

"It's a job. I lay people to rest. Their families get closure, they grieve, they move on. End of story. Anyhow, why the sudden interest to make small talk with me? You've giving me the silent treatment all day. You can't just strike up a conversation with me whenever you like."

"Who said I was giving you the silent treatment? I was staying out of your way like you wanted and at work I have to maintain my cover." He said in a leveled tone.

"Sure." I said quickly. I then turned my head and looked out the window. At that moment, I wished that Michael,

Clarabel or her boyfriend would appear and just shoot me. I seriously had no idea anymore what to feel about Michael, let alone Castor. Anne and Serenity were maybe right but they had no idea how I felt about Castor and there was no way I was going to let anybody know how I felt about him. How was I supposed to deliver myself from temptation when it lived across the hall from me now?

19

We reached Club Thingy a little before ten. I saw Marc, Elijah, Sarah and Anne chugging beers. Angelo was dancing with Sophia. Uncle James was at another table talking to two female administratives from work. I could see the newbies were enjoying themselves. I went up to Marc and kissed him on the cheek. The three tables were a bit crowded, so Marc offered me his lap. I was no longer annoyed with him. Sarah was sitting on Elijah's. I ordered a Cabernet Sauvignon. I wasn't in the mood for drinking but there was no way I was letting anyone know about last night's adventure. *I could see the title of the story: Drunken Damsel in Distress saved by Agent Adonis.*

For the first time, in so long, I was enjoying myself. Anne and a newbie were busting moves on the dance floor. Castor was nowhere to be seen. *Good riddance.* I no longer wanted to swim in a quarry of confusion. I saw Uncle James bring in the birthday cake. We all sang Happy Birthday to Angelo. He was very touched by his cufflinks. He hugged each one of us. The cake was to die for, and I wasn't going to ask who made it. The whole evening was quite uneventful; Michael-free and Castor- free. I didn't see him once. He was probably at the bar.

Anne was discussing the difference between satin and sateen with Sarah and Marc. I was unable to follow. I needed to take a trip to the ladies' room. My bladder quarreled in desperation. I had drunk my body weight in water today. The bathroom was crowded. I managed to go in and out quickly. On my way, back to the crowd, I heard someone call my name.

"Polly?!" I lifted my head up and it was him.

"Is that you? My God! You look gorgeous. How's it going?" He continued loudly over the blaring of the fast-paced music.

"I'm fine and you don't look so bad yourself." I smiled.

Matteo was my second serious relationship. It had only lasted six months. Come to think of it now, I was surprised he even acknowledged my presence. I forgot how handsome he was. I bet he had a piano recital here in the city. Matteo was always travelling around the world. He half smiled and hugged me, tight. He was one of the most affectionate people I'd ever had met. A river of emotion rushed through me. Matteo had been a good friend of mine for a year before we even started dating.

"So, are you here alone?" He asked hopefully.

"As a matter of fact, it's Angelo's birthday. Everyone's here, including Anne."

"So, where's Michael?" He wasn't into being subtle when it came to Michael.

"He's not here. In fact, I haven't seen him in quite a while. He's moved."

"He moved? To where?" He half-snickered.

"Here and there, I didn't ask."

"I understand. You guys had a fallout?"

"Kind of. Can we not talk about him? He's history. I don't think our friendship will be able to survive after that."

"I see." He nodded his head understandingly.

"So, who did you come here with?" I changed the subject.

"Some guys from the orchestra. I'm back home now for a while."

"That's good. Look, I have to get back to my friends."

"Oh, sure. Send my regards to Anne. Catch you later." He gave me another big long hug. Ok, that was a bit too comfortable. I had to break it.

I paced back to my table. Marc and Sarah called it a night. Angelo was now dancing with Anne. Uncle James dragged me to the dance floor, although he was around fifty, he didn't look a day older than thirty-five. He could easily pass for my boyfriend. *I am thirty. Yes, my parents had me at a young age.* I digress. Even when Uncle James was thirty-five, he looked ten years younger. Must be the excessive use of eyeliner and moderate sun exposure. During my teen years, many of my friends at school used to think that I had an older boyfriend. I had never bothered to correct them. It kept losers away from me and Uncle James was more than delighted. Come to think of it, I was surprised that Uncle James was still single. I never knew anything about his personal life other than he lived a very gothic and serene lifestyle.

He twisted and twirled me around the dance floor. He was always a smooth dancer. One of the administrators cut in. I was glad because I didn't think my legs had another dance in them. I saw Matteo come up to me out of the crowd. He asked me to dance with him and I didn't refuse. We danced for five minutes till a slow song came up; I tried to excuse myself, but he just held my hand. He pulled me closer to him holding one hand and grabbing my waist with the other. We swayed and waltzed around. It felt too intimate, too familiar, too comfortable. I felt safe and sound. No terrorists, no guns, no FBI agents on steroids, no abnormal reality.

We danced around as if we were two professional dancers showing the crowd how it's done. I knew a thing or two about dancing, but it was nothing compared to learning the waltz from Matteo. He was a natural and very refined. The only downfall to my relationship with him was that he didn't approve of my career and my macabre lifestyle- and Michael. I think he had used Michael as a reason. He couldn't accept the fact that I was different in many ways.

I pulled back.

"I'm so happy that we danced together. I must go now. You know, graveyard shifts and all. I hope to see you perform soon."

"That's it?" he breathed out sharply.

"Yes, Matteo. Am I missing something?"

Here we go.

"Can we talk at least before you go? There are so many things that I need to say to you. Can we go out and talk?"

"It is what it is. I just didn't love you *that much*." Those last two words were what he used to say to me. *You just don't love me that much.* I put my hand on his cheek. He sighed yet led me outside with the hand that I had placed on his cheek.

"I'm all ears. Say what you need to say but this is just us bumping into each other. It's a one-time thing." *It's either lectures or shrinkery nowadays with me.*

"Polly, I have not gone out with a single girl ever since we broke up. I still think about you all the time. I have even started listening to the music you like sometimes just to understand you better. I now understand that your job isn't easy and isn't morbid as I thought."

You got that from listening to my music? Really? Are we doing this now? Come on, man! Cut me some slack!

"Matt, we didn't break up. You dumped me just because I wanted to go see Michael on opening night in Venice as I recall. It was something I've always done way before I met you. Other than that, you neither accepted the fact that I wasn't a big fan of every classical white-haired bore, nor the fact that I made a career out of burying people. I'd accepted every fault that you had because that's what people who love each other do. What I considered a career, you considered a fault."

"So, that means you did love me '*that much*'." He softly smirked knowing that this was a secret code reference for almost every fight.

"I did. Oh Lord, I did. But you just had to go and set hurdles. I don't do well with complexities. Don't make this anymore hard than it already is on me, please." I was pleading at this point. I meant every word. I didn't need him adding insult to injury. My mental state of mind could not withstand this.

His eyes got a bit misty. He looked like a kid whose mother told him that the tooth fairy was Ozzy Osbourne and that Santa Clause was part of a cult. I saw his eyes shift from me to something behind me.

"Polly, is everything alright? Mr. Roberts told me he saw you leave the club with someone." I turned to find Castor behind me. I turned to introduce them to break the goddamn tension.

"Charles, this is Matteo. Matteo, this is my mother's little cousin Charles." They nodded at each other and shook hands.

"Matteo, it was nice talking to you. Look, I must go back inside and head home with my cousin. Hope to catch you at one of your recitals."

"Oh, you bet I will. I know your address and phone number. I'll mail you the tickets and will expect to see you." He smiled. I knew that was his way of telling me that this conversation is not over. *But, really? What's there to talk about? He broke up with me. I will never admit it to Anne. Fucking Shrinkery.*

"Thanks." He gave me a big hug and kissed my hand. Castor just stood there like a statue. Matteo went back inside, and I was left there standing with Castor outside the club. He handed me my bag and walked with me to the car. He started laughing by himself. I couldn't help but ask what was so funny. I wasn't the least bit amused about his mirth.

"You dated Matteo Harper?" Insinuating the obvious.

"Yes, I did. What's it to you?"

"We catered for a party at his parents' house once. They are filthy rich, stuck up snobs who couldn't tell the difference between tapas and an amuse bouche."

"And you know the difference?" I cocked an eyebrow.

"Of course, I do. Those people spend money on everything but good taste."

"Well, I'll give you credit for that one. Not a big fan of the blown glass chandelier in the foyer. I've seen broken beer bottles that had more class."

"Hahahahaha! So, why did you guys break up?" He was prodding now. It could go either way. *If I involuntarily smack him, it isn't my fault, ok? That is how my reflexes work.*

"It was a bit of everything. He couldn't just accept me for who I am, and you know there was Michael, blah, blah. Other than that, he had always been the perfect gentleman with me. It just didn't work out."

"How long were you guys dating?" Prodding again.

"Six months."

"And where does Michael fit in?" My hand was twitching.

I had told him about Michael's opening night in Venice and how Matteo had a recital and how he dumped me. The whole Bold and the Beautiful soap opera sobfest.

"So, he actually broke up with you because he didn't approve of your ways and used Michael as an alibi?"

"You can put it that way. Michael was the final nail in the coffin."

"Moron." He chuckled. I had ignored that last comment. My palm did not twitch after that.

After that night, things started to fall in place bit by bit with Castor. He wasn't getting in my way and I was staying out of his. There had been a couple of breakthroughs with Michael's case. I hadn't heard from him since the last time I saw him. Castor had made himself quite at home. Sandy came to see him from time to time. I was still going to Serenity's shop after work to pick up his books or help her with the accounting. Anne was traveling to Europe on business for two weeks. My father had gone with her. Lieutenant Prique had given him time-off and he was in dire need of it. He hadn't had a vacation ever since mom died. We all knew that the only reason he took time off because he didn't want Anne traveling alone.

I was working overtime at the graveyard so I wouldn't have to spend so much time with Castor at home. Anyways, Uncle James needed me, Castor, Angelo and the newbies because the two sites he had acquired needed a lot attention. I was working almost twelve hours a day. Uncle James made sure that we got overtime. I couldn't wait to see our end of year bonuses.

In the course of two weeks, my team and I had turned the Saharan grave site into a gothic winter wonderland. The snow had covered all the mausoleums and clear ice drops covered the angelic statues' faces, as if they were crying. The tall trees that the landscaping company had planted were covered in white puffs.

"You outdid yourself, kid" Uncle James put a hand on my shoulder and lightly pinching my cheek as if I were still 6 years old.

"Thanks Uncle James, you're not too shabby yourself." I reciprocated the cheek pinch.

"I'm glad we installed those boulders near the iron fence."

"Yeah, true dat. I'm glad it snowed though. It makes things seem more peaceful."

"Castor did a great job with Angelo. The guy is a lean, mean digging machine. I underestimated him."

"Yeah, he says that you don't acquire such fine skills at FBI school."

"No, you don't" he chuckled.

"I'm going to take some pictures to put on the website. I'll meet you at the parlor in a while."

"Castor will be arriving in a few minutes. I have a funeral to get to." He gave me a hug and left.

Uncle James had spent many summers teaching me about photography. He had taken some courses at school when he was majoring in interior design. I probably had taken over forty pictures of the cemetery. It had been an hour since Uncle James left and Castor hadn't arrived yet. He's never late. Uncle James had made sure that Castor didn't try any funny business with me while my father was gone. Speaking of funny business, Uncle James had made Castor explain to Elijah the effects of gutting someone alive, *you know, just for fun.*

"Where have you been? I'm almost done."

"I was here the whole time. I just didn't want to interrupt you. You seemed so immersed. I brought a thermos of black coffee." He held up the thermos smiling. He was also holding a big paper bag, *mmm...something sweet?*

"You were lurking here the whole time? That's just weird and stalker-like of you."

"Well, I enjoyed watching you enjoying yourself. Frankly, I was looking at the whole cemetery. We did great, didn't we?"

"Yeah, I'm so glad you talked Uncle James into specializing an area for Pagans and Wiccans. Gotta love those Elven stars and triquetras you had Angelo carve. You've increased our clientele by ten percent because of this."

"Angelo wasn't too happy at first, being an Italian Catholic and not knowing any better. But he's a fast learner."

"It was Uncle James' decision eventually." I smiled.

We sat down next to an archangel's pedestal. Its wings hovered over the center of the cemetery. It was the biggest effigy in the whole place. Castor poured me a cup of black coffee. It was getting dark and the halogens automatically went on. We just stared at the place and it was so quiet. There was a deafening silence. I could hear the sound of my own heart beating. The trees were rustling, and the zephyr was so chilling, I could feel my organs gradually freeze.

"Here, have a doughnut. I haven't seen you leave the house for one in weeks." He offered me a chocolate glazed doughnut.

"Eating cheesecakes and strawberry tarts has curbed my doughnut cravings."

"Yeah, I do make one hell of a cheesecake and a heart-stopping strawberry tart." He laughed.

"I think I'm done for now. Can we go home? I think a storm is coming. Nevertheless, I want to be home in time for when Anne and my dad call."

"Here, I went shopping today and got you this jacket. It's padded and has pleather sleeves. It may not be your liking, but it will keep you warm. That trench doesn't keep you warm."

"Well, thanks. You shouldn't have. I didn't have the time to go shopping. You know, with the sugar comas."

"Yeah, *that's* the reason." He laughed.

I put the jacket on. It felt so great not to feel the urine passing from my kidneys to my bladder. Castor was trying not be a jerk. I had to give him credit.

"So, let's go. You don't want to miss Anne or Johnny. Maybe Sandy will swing by later. He misses me. Is Serenity coming over tonight?"

"I think she is. Why are you asking?"

"So, I don't put vinegar in the salad dressing." He rolled his eyes and scoffed.

"Good call." I pursed my lips.

We made our way through the cemetery. Castor was explaining to me how the String theory is the theory of everything. I was easily processing his conjectures about it.

Suddenly, he grabbed my arm and stood motionless. He put a finger on my mouth. Everything went dead still. I knew something was wrong. He motioned with his hand for me to walk with him into one of the mausoleums.

He put both hands on my shoulders. "Polly, somebody is out there. I need you to stay near me and never leave my sight no matter what." He whispered. He texted someone, for back-up, *I think*. I saw him remove a gun from under his overall. The whole time I've known Castor, I had never seen him handle a weapon of any sort, except for that day on the bus- that was different. I couldn't help but feel a bit anxious.

"Is that a Glock 19, as in law enforcement issue?" I stuttered.

"Yes. I didn't know you knew about weapons."

"Dad's friends spend too much time at our place."

His phone vibrated. He had received a message. He frowned and was silent for a second. "Polly,intel has reported that Michael may be here. I think he's in disguise, blonde hair and blue eyes."

"Why would he come here? What does he want?" My

stomach was about to leap out of my damn throat. I may need a paper bag.

"I have no idea but whatever it is, it can't be good." *No shit.*

"How do you know?"

"From the message, he conveyed to me last time in Russian."

"Yeah, you never translated that for me."

"I know and I shouldn't. Now's not the time. You stay here I'm just going to look around."

"I thought you called for back-up. By the by, how are they sure that it may be Michael here?" *And why would the idiot be in the same blonde hair and blue-eyed guise? Dumbass.*

"Like I told you, some of our newbies are FBI agents and one of them suspected something unusual today that's why I had James send you here, so Michael doesn't suspect anything. This way we don't subject the other employees to danger. Don't worry, everyone at this cemetery is FBI, even the grounds-keeper."

My head just spun out of control. He walked out the mausoleum and I saw him motion to the other 'undertakers' to march towards the archangel. I couldn't believe the people I had bossed around for the past few weeks were in fact agents. They were so good and believable at their jobs. After a few moments, I heard something that sounded like a zipper, a zipper on steroids with amplifiers. I looked out and saw two agents laying on the ground face down. They were writhing in their own blood on the snow. We were being ambushed.

Castor came back in and took me by my hand. He dragged me to the back of the mausoleum. I had no idea what was going on. I saw from where the zipper sound came from; behind the tree next to the archangel. It was a heavy machine gun called a Dushka, if I wasn't mistaken, and it was imploding its wrath everywhere.

"Polly, I need you to run towards the grey-stoned seraph on the other side!"

"What about you?!"

"I've got your back. Three of my men are down, there are five left, one of them is waiting for you over there. He has orders to take you out of here. Don't worry about me! Don't look back! Go! Go!" He hollered over the sounds of shots fired.

I turned and ran as fast as I could. I made believe like I was running away from the color pink. I tried to maintain my breathing the same way Coach Nathan had taught me during high school. I could hear the exchange of gunshots behind me. I didn't even look back because Castor told me not to. I had almost reached the seraph and when I saw an agent there. He was wearing goggles and a wool hat. He motioned with his hand to keep moving towards him. I ran around the seraph's pedestal to get to him. He grabbed me when I almost tripped getting to him. Well, I almost tripped because there was a dead body on the floor oozing with blood and stripped of its clothes. I looked up at the agent and there was a smirk which brought back foolish memories.

"Let go of me!" I yelled.

"I'll shoot you, I swear!" He threatened.

Michael held me and turned my back to him. The bastard was going to use me as a human shield. I saw Castor appear. He had been shot in the shoulder. I saw a few FBI agents moving in on us. Michael cocked his gun and put it to my head.

"I'll shoot her! I swear!" *I mean, reword your threats for crying out loud! All the movie quotes he could have used.* I was internally shaking my head and trying not to mess myself.

"FBI! Put your gun down and release the girl!" Castor yelled.

"I'm not!"

I felt a hot flash of tears down my cold cheeks. Michael was gripping me so tight, I thought that he was going to crack my ribs. How the hell did that Primadonna ballerina get such abnormal upper body strength? *Never mind my dumb question.* I had never seen Michael so crazed in my life. I was literally being held hostage by someone I didn't recognize. If only I could move or hit him in some way. I was reviewing the hand to hand combat techniques I had watched on TV. *Okay, this was Dad's fault. He never taught me hand to hand combat. He and his stupid steaks. I was going to die with a chocolate donut in my belly.*

Michael cut off my string of thoughts with sticking the gun's barrel to my clavicle. You idiot -stick with the head, you'd have a better chance of killing me. Castor didn't make any eye contact with me. His eyes were the whole time on Michael. His eyes then shifted from Michael to the sound of a helicopter over our heads. They were shooting as us.

I elbowed Michael to distract him to no avail. Castor was running towards us trying to avoid being shot. I started thinking about how all heroes in those Hollywood movies cheat death like fifty times. I'm never watching movies again. There wasn't going to be any retakes here because Castor got gunned down. I stomped on Michael's instep thus turning while freeing myself only for him to shoot me three times in the chest. *Overkill, much?* It happened all so fast. *Oh crap, not again.*
I hope I die this time.

How many times can a person die? Metaphorically? Literally? Dying metaphorically is never-ending hell; dying literally happens only once. Or so I thought. Everything I knew disappeared in an instant. My faith in science and religion was shaken.

A black weight was dragging me down and down, washing over me like a subtle wave. I was expecting to see the cliché 'white light at the end of the tunnel', but then I didn't. Was Nietzsche, right? Was there such a thing as annihilation? If this was it, then boy was it peaceful.

All I could hear was death and all I could see was nothing. Yet, I felt everything. I wish I hadn't had that doughnut. I still couldn't believe that I could actually feel heartburn even now.

I was waiting to see my mom. But she wasn't there. *Somebody please?!* Dead person crossing over! My mother was right. When someone dies, they think of the person they love the most. One regret though, if I knew what was best for me, I would've fallen in love with someone like him. I hope I'd be able to take away with me the musky rosy smell that I once adored. I heard the same voice in my ear when I got shot the first time; '*everything's going to be alright*' and it was because I went numb and felt nothing no more.

I was home.

Follow me on Instagram for updates on the upcoming book at **mj.author**.

Made in the USA
Columbia, SC
04 June 2025

58382268R00119